TO DIE FOR

Catherine Jinks was born in Brisbane, Australia, in 1963. She grew up in Papua New Guinea and later spent four years studying medieval history at the University of Sydney. After leaving university, she worked as a journalist, and her first book was published in 1991. She now writes full-time and is the award-winning author of novels for both children and adults. She lives in the Blue Mountains, Australia, with her husband, Peter, and their daughter. TO DIE FOR is her first novel for Macmillan Children's Books.

TO DIE FOR

Catherine Jinks

MACMILLAN CHILDREN'S BOOKS

First published 2000 by Pan Macmillan Australia Pty Limited

First published in the UK 2002 by Macmillan Children's Books
a division of Macmillan Publishers Ltd
20 New Wharf Road, London N1 9RR
Basingstoke and Oxford
www.panmacmillan.com

Associated companies throughout the world

ISBN 0 330 399187

1 3 5 7 9 8 6 4 2

A CIP catalogue record for this book is available from
the British Library.

Typeset in Sabon by SX Composing DTP, Rayleigh, Essex
Printed and bound in Great Britain by Mackays of Chatham plc, Chatham, Kent

To my darling husband, Peter, without whom this book would never, ever have been written.

What's Hector McKerrow doing these days? Can anyone tell me?

Hi. My name is Mercy Whetton, I live in Nova Scotia, and I created this message board to find out what I can about Hector McKerrow. I *love* Hector McKerrow. And most people don't even know who he is!

Has anyone else in the world been watching *The Family Way*, at 1.30 a.m. Tuesdays, on the Nickelodeon channel? I only found it myself because I was recording another show, and let the tape run to its end. But now I'm recording every episode. *The Family Way* is an old 1960s series about a mad scientist called Dr Devlin, who's moved to a typical American town with his family. Trouble is, his family isn't like other families. His wife, Sylvia, is a robot. His younger son, Troy, is an alien wearing a suit that makes him look like a small boy. And his daughter, Dixie, is a little like Frankenstein – only prettier – because she's been put together from pieces of dead bodies. Dr Devlin has made a home for all of these people so that his elder son, Zac, will have a proper family. Zac's mother died when he was young, you see, and Dr Devlin couldn't raise a child all on his own.

It's a very funny series. It can be pretty clever, too. But the best thing about it is Zac Devlin, who's played by Hector McKerrow. Zac is *so cute*. I guess he's supposed to be about eighteen – and I want to know if Hector McKerrow was the same age, at that time. Or was he older? I've never seen him in anything else, even though I watch a lot of old-time movies. In *The Family Way*, he's a real rebel, always disobeying rules and riding around on a motorbike and wearing a leather jacket. (In the first episode, there was a big fight about his leather jacket. It's hard to believe that leather jackets were like smoking, once, or like hanging out with junkies.) Anyways, for those who haven't seen him, he has dark hair and long eyelashes and a soft, rough voice, and he is *to die for*. I love him. I want to send him a letter, wherever he is, and tell him so.

Does anyone know how I can find him?

Subject: I see that you're not exactly flooded
Sender: s.o.inoz – 4.03 p.m. February 12

I see that you're not exactly flooded with replies, Mercy Whetton. Let me guess: you're about ten, right? And your parents helped you to set up this message board? Well, you're in the wrong place, kiddo. You should be in the Leonardo di Caprio chat room, or the *NSYNC web page. I can guarantee that no one else is drooling over a 1960s comedy star who only surfaces at 1.30 a.m.

As for me, I'm fifteen, I live in Australia, and I don't have access to Canadian TV channels. The only reason I happen to have watched just one (count it, *one*) episode of *The Family Way* is because my cousin works for the film and video library of a local TV station, here in Sydney. Occasionally, when the clan gathers at my grandmother's house to celebrate Christmas, or birthdays, or the fact that we haven't all killed each other yet, my cousin will produce a clutch of 'wacky old stuff' (his phrase) for our general amusement. I wouldn't say that this ploy is wholly successful, because there are generally so many fights going on among the crumpled gift wrapping that the video player can't compete. But at least I get exposed to more programs than a girl without access to cable television can usually expect to see. Like *The Family Way*, for instance.

As I said, I've only watched the first episode of this series. What I saw, however, was enough to convince me that *The Family Way* is going to become the topic of my next Media Studies project. We have to – and I quote my teacher Mrs Skerman – 'look at how one television program, series or ad campaign reflects the current social trends and the competing demands of audience, marketers, and programmers'. (Notice how unclear her wording is. By 'current social trends' does she mean today's social trends, or the social trends of the time in which the program was made?) Now it just so happens that I don't want to admit, in writing, that I've watched any particular soap or police show or English dramatized classic made in the last two years, because what if Mrs Skerman decides to discuss our projects in class? I'd spend the rest of the year saying, over and over again, 'No, I don't watch *Days of Our Lives* regularly, it was just for the project.' God forbid that I should be classified as a fan of any show that puts me in the same category as a bunch of deadheads.

So I've decided to use *The Family Way*. Since no one else in Australia (outside my family) can have watched *The Family Way* during the last twenty years, or whatever – because it's not on pay TV here, I've checked – I'm quite safe in choosing it. I also happen to think that it's a great subject, because it predicts exactly what's going to happen to the nuclear family in the next millennium. You've got a father utterly obsessed with his work, who hardly ever emerges from his basement lab; you've got one kid who's not only alienated, but literally *an alien*; you've got a girl who's obsessed with her body, and whether her hips are too big compared to her shoulders (only she's got an excuse, because all her parts come from entirely different people); and you've got a mother who's just a piece of technology. There must be millions of kids, these days, who are brought up by televisions, microwave ovens, mobile phone and computers. I think *The Family Way* is a very insightful examination of the breakdown of blood relationships in the modern era. At least, that's what I'm going to tell Mrs Skerman.

Is there any way you can give me a description of each episode, as they broadcast it? That way I'll know what I'm talking about.

Subject: Sure I'll tell you
Sender: mercynova – 4.20 p.m. February 12

Sure, I'll tell you about each episode as soon as I've watched it. But you're wrong about me. I'm twelve, not ten. And I hate the *NSYNC. And I wasn't raised by a microwave, and we don't have a mobile. My family hasn't broken up. I see a lot of my dad – he takes me tobogganing. (He used to take my sister, until she turned sixteen and stopped wanting to go.) He also taught me how to ride a bike. My mom showed me how to make banana muffins, and takes me to all the figure-skating shows in Halifax. (We live in Greenwood.) Last summer, we went camping in Cape Breton for two weeks.

I don't think you're right about the nuclear family in the next millennium. I don't want to be rude, but it sounds like you might be thinking about your own family. Are you mad at your mom? Or your dad? I don't think *The Family Way* is about families breaking up, because Zac and Dixie and Sylvia and Troy and even Dr Devlin all love each other a lot. They may fight sometimes (except for Sylvia, who never fights), but they love each other. Even Zac, who knows that his family are a bunch of weird outcasts and thinks that he'll never get a girlfriend because of them, hates it when people are mean to Sylvia, or Dixie, or Troy.

You didn't tell me what you thought about Zac. He's wonderful, isn't he? I love the way he narrows his beautiful blue eyes when he's waiting for someone to say something stupid. I wonder if he's alive or dead? I wish I could find out.

Subject: As far as I'm concerned Zac is only interesting
Sender: s.o.inoz – 8.14 a.m. February 13

As far as I'm concerned, Zac is only interesting because he manages to look a bit tough even though he's on a 1960s comedy show. I haven't seen many 1960s comedy shows, but if *I Dream of Jeannie* and *The Brady Bunch* are anything to go by, main characters don't usually say nasty things about high school proms, the way Zac did in the episode I saw. I can't help thinking that *The Family Way* must have been pretty unusual. Some of the humour is quite black. And most of the other 1960s television families seem to spend their time camping, biking, cooking muffins . . . wait! Hang on. Does that sound familiar to you?

For your information, mercynova, my own family doesn't go camping. My mother probably isn't aware that there is such a thing as a non-electric tin-opener. My brother is too busy smoking dope, and hanging around shopping centre car parks, to find the time for an extended hike through the Royal National Park. As for my father, I don't think he actually exists. I think he's really the voice of our answering machine. Even when he lived here, he was just a smell in the bathroom and an enormous dry-cleaning bill.

Just because Zac hates it when people attack Sylvia, or Troy, or Dixie, it doesn't necessarily mean that he loves them. He might mean simply that an attack on them is like an attack on him.

Subject: What's your real name
Sender: mercynova – 8.34 p.m. February 12

What's your real name, s.o.inoz? You sound so miserable. I'm sorry your home isn't very happy, but that doesn't mean you should be calling my family the Brady Bunch!

The Devlins do love each other. In the last episode, Zac was expelled for playing hooky, and because it was the school's football coach who caught him at it he spiked the team's linament with some kind of itchy stuff. Not only was the big game threatened, but Dixie's long-awaited date with one of the players was cancelled. She was very unhappy, and she knew that Zac was responsible because he'd been experimenting on the family dog. When she accused him of ruining her life, he felt bad. In fact he felt so bad that he confessed to his father, because he wanted his father to help him invent a cure for the itch. He wouldn't have done that if he didn't love Dixie.

Don't you think that Hector McKerrow was more interesting (not to mention better looking) than most of the young guys on TV today?

Subject: Since most of the young guys on TV today
Sender: s.o.inoz – 4.40 p.m. February 13

Since most of the young guys on TV today look and act like animated blobs of hair gel, as depicted on laminated bubblegum cards, I would have to say that yes, Hector McKerrow was, in many ways, a superior product. But he was just a product, mercynova. His lines were written by somebody else, and you can bet that he wasn't responsible for his wardrobe, or his hairstyle, or his make-up.

My name, by the way, is Adamina. You might ask yourself: what kind of a name is that? And my answer to you is: the kind of name dreamed up by a woman, out of her head on pethidine, who has just given birth in a Broken Hill hospital. Adamina means 'red earth', you see, and there is plenty of red earth in Broken Hill. There are also plenty of mines – or there used to be. My father, I should tell you, is a mining executive. He's always pissing off to remote places where no one likes Greenpeace, and where the only souvenirs you can find are bits of rock. I've got quite a collection of bits of rock. Twenty-three bits of rock, dumped in a box under my bed. Hell, who needs phoney Reeboks, or Florentine writing paper, or a shell necklace? Just give me a nice chunk of rock to put under my bed.

Subject: My name is neville
Sender: keyop.1 – 12.12 p.m. February 13

My name is Neville, and I saw *The Family Way* when it first went to air, here in the UK; I was twelve years old at the time. I thought it an exceptional series, and still do, though it obviously failed to attract a large audience. Were you aware that the NBC made only one season's worth of episodes? That was in 1967, though they were screened here in 1968. The series was billed as a cross between *The Addams Family* and *My Favorite Martian*, but I think it was more than that. I think it had a touch of genius.

You must be wondering where I got all this information. Well, the fact is, I have before me an ancient cardboard envelope, stuffed full of clippings that I collected on the subject of *The Family Way* and its performers, when I was twelve. I know, for example, that Hector McKerrow was twenty years old in 1968; that Zac Devlin was his third television role; that in 1965 he appeared in one episode of a series called *Camp Runamuck* (he played a homesick inmate of a boys' summer camp), and that in 1966 he was featured in the third episode of *Dark Shadows*, playing a teenage ghoul of some kind. Unfortunately, I never saw either of these shows. Nor did I ever witness his brief appearances in *Felony Squad* (1968), *Ironside* (1968), *The FBI* (1968), or *Dragnet* (1969), though I believe that he was somewhat typecast as a tough, teenage punk. The last piece of information I have on him mentions a film that he was to star in, scheduled for production in 1970.

I also seem to recall that he was involved in a small scandal, but can find no reference to it among my clippings. As far as I can remember, it involved a fight over a girlfriend. No girlfriend is named in the articles and interviews that I currently possess, but that isn't surprising. John Lennon's first wife was a well-kept secret for some time, and Hector McKerrow must have been viewed as a possible pin-up boy. It's nice to see that girls like you, Mercy, are as enthusiastic about him now as they were in 1968. My own girlfriend was an avid fan, until some unmemorable pop star dislodged Hector from his pre-eminent place in her heart.

I, myself, was more attracted to Dixie, played by one Rosemary Deeble. Rosemary was twenty-two when she assumed the part of seventeen-year-old Dixie; at the age of twenty, she had scored her first TV role as a bikini-clad extra in *Gidget*. She was also in *Dr Kildare* (1966) – probably as a coma victim – and in something called *The Young Marrieds* (1965), as somebody's visiting sister.

In case you're interested, Ralph Endacott, who played Troy, had already appeared in *Lassie* (1966) and *My Mother the Car* (1966), which was about – you won't believe this – a man who heard his late mother's voice emanating from a vintage car. Myron Landers, who played Dr Prosper Devlin in *The Family Way*, was a veteran actor who had appeared in many old movies, including a lot of Westerns (he usually played a judge, or doctor – I've seen him in a few), as well as a handful of funny old shows like *The Alfred Hitchcock Hour* and *Maverick*. Sylvia's face, as it appears on the television screen between her metallic shoulders, is the face of Ida Blount, who was in quite a few B-grade movies during the 1950s, and who also scored a role in *The Flying Nun* in 1968.

I hope this satisfies your desire for more information, Mercy. Perhaps it will also help Adamina in her project. I just want to add, Mercy, that you shouldn't be publicizing your surname and home town all over the Internet. Someone could easily find out where you live.

Subject: You keep old clippings
Sender: s.o.inoz – 7.45 a.m. February 14

You keep old clippings from when you were *twelve*? Keyop.1, I'm not too good at maths, but if you were twelve in 1968, that means you're forty-four now. You must have led a *very* unexciting life.

Subject: Thank you very much
Sender: mercynova – 5.48 p.m. February 13

Thank you very much, Neville. Do you think you could photocopy those articles for me? I'll pay for the photocopying, and for the postage. I would love to have a picture of Hector McKerrow. Can you remember the name of the film that he was going to star in?

Subject: I can't believe it
Sender: zinglebrit – 7.11 p.m. February 13

I can't believe it! Someone else is watching *The Family Way*! I *totally* love that show. I am *crazy* for Zac. I adore his long, skinny legs in those tight jeans! And the way he wraps them around the sofa cushions! (Groan.) God, I'm like, how can fate be so cruel? At last I've discovered my soul mate, and he's gotta be forty years older than I am!

Mercy, I know just how you feel. But don't despair, because my dad is a lawyer for Universal Pictures. He tells me that to find an actor you have to contact the Screen Actors' Guild, and someone there will know who the guy's agent or manager is. So that's what I'm going to do. No big deal. I'll find out what Hector McKerrow is doing these days, and you can send him a letter. Hey – if he lives here in LA (and most of 'em do), I might even deliver it myself.

By the way, what that English guy said about the fight over the girlfriend was interesting. Just what you'd expect from Hector. Do you think he's part Latino? His hair sure is dark enough. Though what they say about temperamental Latinos is a total crock – the most gentle guy I ever went out with was from Cuba. And the only guy who ever got into a fight over me was a grade-A Ivy League WASP.

Subject: I'd be happy to send you
Sender: keyop.1 – 11.03.a.m. February 14

I'd be happy to send you copies of everything I have, Mercy – and don't worry about the expense. I think I can afford it more easily than you. But before you e-mail me your postal address (and my e-mail is prattboss@unus.com.uk), you should check with your parents. They may not want you to contact me. Or they might want to speak to me themselves, first.

The film that I mentioned was entitled *Last Summer Blues*. I don't know anything else about it, except that Hector was supposed to be one of the stars.

Subject: Give me a break
Sender: s.o.inoz – 12.05 p.m. February 15

Give me a break, zinglebrit. You live in Los Angeles, your father works for Universal Pictures, you've got a million boyfriends, and you're sitting around reading message boards like this on the Internet? Please.

The Internet is for antisocial losers like me and Neville. People who hardly ever emerge from their dark, untidy rooms. People who don't have any *real* friends. People who don't play sport, who are addicted to computer games, and who are either a) cursed with enormous IQs, together with disfiguring acne, or b) planning to massacre half the kids at their school.

Don't give me all that garbage about Cubans. If there really were any Cubans in your life, you'd be out raging with them right now. Isn't it St Valentine's Day where you are?

14

Subject: I'm not an antisocial loser
Sender: mercynova – 9.15 p.m. February 14

I'm not an antisocial loser, and I'm not planning to massacre half the kids at my school. The reason I'm on the Internet is that it's winter here in Canada, and there's snow falling outside. You can only spend so much time in the snow, Adamina. After a while, your hands go numb.

Subject: You're right
Sender: keyop.1 – 12.02 p.m. February 15

You're right, Adamina. I *am* addicted to computer games. I don't play sport. And I wear glasses, on top of everything else. How's that for a loser?

Subject: As a matter of fact
Sender: zinglebrit – 5.16 p.m. February 15

As a matter of fact, s.o.inoz, I play basketball sometimes, though not as much as I used to. But who cares? The important thing is that I called the Screen Actors' Guild today, and found out that Hector McKerrow doesn't have an agent or manager any more. All they could give me was a phone number, and that turned out to be disconnected. But I did get the name of Hector's former agent. She told me he hasn't worked since 1991 – she doesn't know what he's doing now. But she faxed me his details, and *boy*, what a sad case. Nothing but pilots and bit parts. Coma victims, like poor old Rosemary Deeble. God. It's totally tragic.

Adamina: if you scroll down a little, you'll notice that I've scanned in a shot of me and the Cuban, whose name is Eduardo. That's him, sitting at the head of the table. I'm beside him, and next to me is the WASP, Philip. At the time, Philip was going out with that flaky-looking girl in the white sweater.

A guy called Jacques took me out on St Valentine's Day, but he's a recent acquisition, so I don't have a photograph yet.

Subject: I could use a few more details
Sender: keyop.1 – 12.38 p.m. February 16

I could use a few more details about Hector for my clippings file, zinglebrit. (Nice handle – it suits your face.) Would you post the contents of that fax on the board, please?

Subject: Please zinglebrit can you tell us more
Sender: mercynova – 4.23 p.m. February 16

Please, zinglebrit, can you tell us more about Hector? What do you mean, pilots and bit parts? I want to know *everything*.

Subject: So you've got a scanner
Sender: s.o.inoz – 7.45 p.m. February 17

So you've got a scanner, zinglebrit? Doesn't surprise me. I suppose it's your own scanner, too, and sits in your bedroom with your Barbie-pink wide-screen TV, your video player, your computer, your stereo system and your exercise machines.

I think that photo is a fake. Why would a blonde California surfer-girl be surfing the Internet when she could be at the beach? (PS Have you had plastic surgery?)

Subject: I surf the internet because
Sender: zinglebrit – 4.45 p.m. February 16

I surf the Internet because it lets me talk to people like you, Adamina – people who don't have their own mobiles and computer scanners and stereo systems. Gives me a sense of *perspective*, you know? I'm like: Thank you, God, that my life is so rich and fortunate, and I haven't become all grouchy and jealous and pissed off, like some people. Oh, and I *haven't* had plastic surgery, because I'm only sixteen. But I can recommend a good surgeon to you, if you're that desperate.

OK, now I'm going to post what I've got here on Hector McKerrow's career. In 1969, he landed a small, two-episode part in a soap called *Bright Promise*, about college kids, and another part as a gunslinger in *Daniel Boone*. He also did a pilot where he starred as the son of a city lawyer who goes back to his home town, and that was called *Soperville*, but it didn't get off the ground. Then in 1970 he was in that movie, *Last Summer Blues*, as the best friend of the hero – so he got second billing. It looks like he stopped playing teenage punks, after a while, and started playing hoods instead – at least, that's the only thing I can figure from all the cop shows he was in: *Adam-12* (1970), *Columbo* (1971), *Mannix*

(1971), *McCloud* (1972), *McMillan and Wife* (1972), *The Rookies* (1972), *Cannon* (1973), *Kojak* (1974), *Harry O* (1974), *Most Wanted* (1976), *Rafferty* (1977), *Richie Brockleman, Private Eye* (1978), *Mrs Columbo* (1979). I can't tell you if he was always the crook in these things. He certainly wasn't one of the leads. Maybe they thought he had a 'Mafia' look, or something. All that shiny black hair, I guess.

He was also in a few westerns and medical shows: *The Interns* (1971), *Medical Center* (1973), *Gunsmoke* (1974), *Kung Fu* (1974), *The Quest* (1976), *Quincy, M.E.* (1977), *The Doctors* (1979). My guess is that he played coma victims and bullet-riddled bodies, poor guy.

He did two more pilots and a movie before 1980. One of the pilots was called *Mob Rule* (1976), and it was a sitcom about mobsters (no wonder it never made the grade), in which he starred as the head gangster's eldest son. The other was a cop show called *Bastian* (1975), in which he played the young rookie partner of the hero, Ed Bastian.

The movie was called *Downside* (1978). He played a drug dealer in it. I saw it, years ago, and I remember that one of the bad guys was found hanging in a meat freezer. So that was probably him.

There were a couple of other series guest spots in the 1970s – *Emergency* (he was probably trapped under a fallen tree), *Monster Squad* (kids' show), and *Wonder Woman*. But in the 1980s he didn't seem to get as much work. No movies. There was *Here's Boomer* (1980), *Concrete Cowboys* (1981), *Matt Houston* (1982), *Masquerade* (1983), *The Love Boat* (1983), *Fantasy Island* (1984), *Cagney and Lacey* (1984), *The A Team* (1984), *The Fall Guy* (1985), and then nothing until 1989, when he did *Miami Vice*. In 1990 he got a part in *Freddy's Nightmares*, and in 1991 he did this movie, *Cranks*. Have you ever seen such a miserable collection? According to Dad's reference books, *Here's Boomer* was a remake of a dog show called *The Littlest Hobo*, *Concrete Cowboys* was about truckers, *Matt Houston* was about a rich Texan amateur detective who was also supervising an offshore oil rig, and *Masquerade* was about a secret agent called Lavender who decided to use ordinary American tourists for overseas missions. I've seen a few episodes of *Freddy's Nightmares*, but I wasn't looking out for Hector McKerrow at the time. He was probably skewered through the eyeball, or something.

I'm going to watch that movie, *Cranks*. It shouldn't be too hard to find. Dad says it was a comedy about eccentric inventors and sank like a stone, but the local video store is about a block long and two blocks wide, so it should be in there somewhere.

Anybody else seen *Cranks*?

Subject: A very thorough job
Sender: keyop.1 – 12.45 a.m. February 17

A very thorough job, zinglebrit. What a nostalgic journey. My eyes positively misted over when they encountered *Kung Fu* and *The A Team*. Unfortunately, I'm not familiar with *Downside* or *Cranks*, but shall scour my local video shop forthwith.

Subject: I've seen cranks
Sender: s.o.inoz – 12.32 p.m. February 17

I've seen *Cranks* – or at least, I've seen about half of it. (My brother has a taste for crap films like that, and used to spend a good deal of time rotting his brain with dumb videos.) If Hector McKerrow was in it, then he must have played the mad inventor in the loony bin, because Ivan Weiss played the hero, and that kid from *Stay Clean* played the young inventor. The mad guy had Albert Einstein hair and weirdo glasses, and his voice was deeper – you wouldn't have recognized him. But it had to be Hector. He was about the right age, for one thing. And he still had those long, skinny legs.

Christ, how depressing. It was such a stupid part. *Here's Boomer* and *Monster Squad* – no wonder he gave it all up nine years ago. I only hope he's made a fortune selling real estate, since then.

Oh well. Life might be a bit of a drag, but at least I was never in *Monster Squad*.

Subject: I don't usually sign up
Sender: mousehound – 10.00 p.m.
February 16

I don't usually sign up for chat rooms or bulletin boards. But I live in the same apartment building as Hector McKerrow's ex-wife, Patty Pryor. So I thought I should say something.

My mother told me Hector and Patty split up years ago, before I was born – and I'm eleven. She told me they used to fight a lot. One time they smashed a window, throwing books and coffee tables about.

Patty Pryor is an actress. My mother says she used to do shows on Broadway.

We live in the west 70s, in New York.

Hi, Adamina, I just finished watching the tape that I made of last night's episode. You know how Dixie wants to be normal and popular, like her friend Sandra next door? Well, last night she decided to try out as a cheerleader. The first scene started with her jumping around the living room, waving her pompoms. And Zac, who was trying to watch TV, said that she was only doing it because cheerleaders date football players. (He *hates* football players!) And they got into a big argument, with him saying that she looked like a crazy poodle, and her saying why couldn't he be normal for once? Then the argument stopped when the dog jumped up, snatched one of Dixie's pompoms out of her hand, and ran away with it.

Maybe you don't know that they have a new dog in each episode. Because ordinary dogs always attack Troy, Dr Devlin has to experiment on strays from the pound, operating on their brains to make them happy and peaceful. But something goes wrong every time. This time the dog kept leaping into the air and snatching things out of people's hands or mouths. In one scene it snatched a cigarette out of Zac's mouth, while he was smoking behind a tree in the yard. (He's not allowed to smoke, see.) Then it ran back into the house, smoking the cigarette. It ran around and around the kitchen, up the stairs, down into the basement, trying to get away from Sylvia and Dr Devlin, who were chasing it. Finally, Sylvia caught it with her supersonic whistle, and a kind of net that blew out of a little hatch on her shoulder. Then the kids were made to stand in line, and Dr Devlin asked them who the cigarette belonged to.

Zac wouldn't own up. I think he's a bit scared of his father. So Dr Devlin warned all three kids that if any of them smoked another cigarette, they'd regret it for the rest of their lives – and was he ever convincing! *I'd* sure be scared of him, if he was *my* dad. After that, he spiked their Koolaid with some kind of chemical, which turned Zac's teeth black as soon as he smoked his next cigarette. But before the Koolaid scene, Zac did something to Dixie's pompoms. (I love the way he's always making gadgets!) He fixed the pompoms so that they were radio controlled, like slot cars, and when she tried out for the cheer squad, he sat outside the gym with his little black box and made the pompoms act like little furry animals. They jerked Dixie's arms around, making her hit people and look stupid, until finally she was disqualified. And that made her very upset.

She was crying when Sylvia picked her up from school. Sylvia promised that Zac would be punished. But by that time Zac had already been punished, because his teeth had turned black. He had to hide away in his room, and not go to Sandra's birthday party. Do you know that he likes Sandra? He was really disappointed to miss her party. And Dixie said that maybe now he knew how she felt, missing out on something important. And that made him feel bad.

To make it up to her, he swapped both of her slot car pompoms for the pompoms of a mean girl called Valerie. You see, the whole cheer squad was at Sandra's party (because Sandra was on the squad), and he could hear them chanting a birthday chant through his bedroom window. So he snuck over to Sandra's house – where Valerie was being horrible to Dixie, saying nasty things

26

about her technique – and swapped the pompoms around while everyone was singing 'Happy Birthday' over the cake. While he was waiting to do this, he overheard Sandra asking Dixie where he was. When Dixie replied that he was sick, Sandra said all kinds of nice things about him. She said that she would keep some cake for him, and deliver it to him herself. Hearing this stuff made him feel so good that he didn't mind missing the party, after all.

At the next cheerleader rehearsal, Valerie's pompoms went mad, and she was expelled from the squad. It was decided that there should be another try-out. Of course, you just *knew* that Dixie would get in. Sure enough, the last scene showed the season's first big football match, with Dixie jumping about, waving her pompoms, and Sandra smiling up at Zac, who was sitting with his family in the stand. He was wearing his leather jacket, but he had a very geeky sweater on his knees. When the ball started to behave weirdly, moving in one direction when it was kicked in another, it became obvious that Zac's little black box was hidden under the sweater on his knees. Thanks to him, the home team stopped losing.

The final shot was of that dumb dog, streaking out on to the field, leaping into the air, grabbing the ball and running away with it.

Bit stupid, really.

Mousehound: do you think Patty Pryor would forward my letter to Hector McKerrow?

Subject: Thanks mercy
Sender: s.o.inoz – 5.08 p.m. February 18

Thanks, Mercy, I appreciate your time. Sounds like an interesting episode. But I should tell you that, from what I know about ex-wives (and I know a lot, because I live with one), there's no way Patty Pryor is going to be saddled with Hector's mail. No way.

Subject: I don't know patty pryor
Sender: mousehound – 8.00 p.m. February 18

I don't know Patty Pryor. I can't give her a letter. I've never even said hello.

Sorry.

Subject: Great episode
Sender: zinglebrit – 6.30 p.m. February 18

Great episode, don't you think? But Sandra is *so* wrong for Zac, I mean check out the eyeliner. What does he see in her? (Aside from the chest, that is.) Zac has gorgeous hands. He smokes a cigarette like he's playing a violin. Very graceful.

Mousehound, have you ever thought of asking Patty Pryor for an autograph? Maybe, if you did that, you could just sort of *work your way around* to asking about Hector.

Gotta go.

Subject: That's a good idea
Sender: mercynova – 8.45 p.m. February 18

That's a good idea. Couldn't you please try it, mouse-hound? All I want to do is express my admiration. Patty can open the letter and read it, if she wants.

Subject: Ex–wives are usually paid alimony
Sender: s.o.inoz – 9.00 a.m. February 20

Ex-wives are usually paid alimony. If Patty is, then she'll know where to find Hector. Maybe someone should check out her bank statements.

Subject: Adamina i don't see
Sender: keyop.1 – 10.45 p.m. February 19

Adamina, I don't see a little smiley face at the end of your last suggestion. You *were* joking, weren't you? In the future, I recommend that you insert a :-) after your jokes, or people are liable to take them seriously, and break the law.

I should report that I tracked down *Cranks*, yesterday, and watched it last night. A big thumbs down. You were right, Adamina – Hector was the one in the nuthouse. Very sad. And very unnerving for yours truly; the ravages of time haven't been kind to me, either. At least Hector had kept all his hair (or was that a wig?). His conversations with the monkeys were, quite simply, toe-curlingly awful. I had to hit the fast forward button.

Downside doesn't seem to be widely available. Maybe I'll see if I can order it off the Internet.

On the subject of the Internet, I did a search for Patty Pryor and found a CD on a music warehouse site, *Come to the Cabaret: Collected Show Tunes, var. artists*. Patty was listed as the singer of one track, 'Broadway Boogie-woogie'. Most interesting.

Subject: Where are you mousehound
Sender: zinglebrit – 6.30 p.m. February 19

Where are you, mousehound? What did you think of my suggestion? You know, I bet Neville would gladly give some of his priceless Hector McKerrow memorabilia to anyone who helps him track down a genuine Hector McKerrow autograph. Isn't that right, Neville? Hey – whoever finally *finds* Hector McKerrow could even win a prize! I've got a *fabulous* Star Wars clock radio here that I've never even taken out of the box. (Promotional merchandising – a free sample that my dad picked up.) Think about it, mousehound. And what's your real name, anyway? Mine's Britt.

Well, I've got a date tonight, but before I go I just want to say that *Cranks* was a Universal picture. And since it was only made nine years ago, my dad's going to speak to the director, if he can, because they know each other. He's going to find out anything he can about Hector McKerrow. So everyone cross your fingers.

Oh, by the way – Adamina's a *girl's* name, right?

Subject: Yes adamina's a girl's name
Sender: s.o.inoz – 4.00 p.m. February 20

Yes, Adamina's a girl's name. Whether I'm a girl, however – at least by your standards – is debatable. I wear Doc Martens. I don't shave my armpits. I don't have any bosom to speak of. I use wallets and backpacks. I spend a lot of time in the library. I don't chase boys.

As for your suggestion about the clock radio, it's very unfair. What hope do I have of winning it, out here at the ends of the earth? You guys have a much better chance. You, Britt, are living in Tinseltown. Mousehound is sitting practically on top of Hector's ex-wife. Neville's presumably earning an income, so he can run up enormous phone bills. But what have I got? Not even pay TV!

Subject: I have no objection
Sender: keyop.1 – 11.05 a.m. February 20

I have no objection to donating a few clippings, if it will help Mercy unburden her heart to her idol. And to prevent you feeling disadvantaged, Adamina, may I suggest that this contest is based on a points system? Points could be earned for any information pertaining to Hector's current whereabouts. For example, should mousehound extract any useful addresses from Patty Pryor, he – or is it she? – would be eligible for a point score. I would recommend: one hundred points for Hector's whereabouts; twenty points for any information regarding his activities since 1991; fifty points for a post-office box number; forty points for a photograph, and so forth. In the end, person who contributed the most effort would win the prize.

You don't need to be living in Hollywood to participate, Adamina. Who's to say that Hector is living there himself? No – all you need is your computer, your telephone, and a decent library. This world is growing smaller by the minute, you know. Australia isn't that far away, any more.

Subject: I just looked up hector's name
Sender: mercynova – 2.19 p.m. February 20

I just looked up Hector's name on the Internet. I found this message board, of course. And I found two other sites, both of them pretty weird. One is at http://www.wow.net/-harass/research.htm. The other is at http://www.rhetorica.symposium.edu.uk/report.htm. I didn't understand either of them. One was about a 'symposium' in Europe, and Hector McKerrow seemed to be the author of a paper on something called Quintilian's Institutes of Oratory. (Does that sound right to anyone?) He was supposed to have 'argued' and 'contested' and 'concluded' things.

The other site was *really* long – page after page – like a small book. It was called 'War on Waves: NIR, ELF and ultrasonics', and it was written by a guy called Maynard Boyer. Like I said, I didn't understand it. Hector's name was right at the end, under 'CONTACTS & FURTHER REFERENCES'. There was a mailing address for someone called Egon Kucyk, of the International Watchdog on Offensive Microwave Weapons, there were a couple of books (*Mega Brain* by Michael Hutchison, *Electromagnetic Interaction with Biological Systems*, by Professor James

Lin), there was the name and e-mail address of the editor of *Enigma* magazine, and there was a website for Hector McKerrow, of the Free Thought Forum. I tried that website, but it doesn't exist any more.

Do you think this could be the same Hector McKerrow?

Subject: I just spoke to patty pryor
Sender: mousehound – 4.24 p.m. February 20

I just spoke to Patty Pryor. I told her my grandma has that CD, *Come to the Cabaret*. I told her I wanted an autograph for my grandma.

She was very nice. Inside her apartment, she has a stack of publicity shots that she signs for people. So she gave me one of those. I told her my mom said she used to be married to an actor called Hector McKerrow. Then I asked her for his autograph as well. But she said she couldn't help me. She doesn't know where he is.

I said thank you, and left. But just as I reached the door she told me that he still sends her money through her lawyer. So maybe the lawyer knows where to find him. She gave me the lawyer's mailing address – I've got it right here.

How many points would I get for this?

Subject: Cool
Sender: mercynova – 6.00 p.m. February 20

Cool! That's great, mousehound. I wish I'd been there. What does she look like? Were there any old photos on the walls? You're so lucky!

Subject: Did she say anything
Sender: s.o.inoz – 11.11 a.m. February 21

Did she say anything about why she and Hector broke up?
And when?

Subject: Of course she didn't say anything
Sender: mousehound – 8.10 p.m. February 20

Of course she didn't say anything about why she and
Hector broke up. What, are you crazy? I've been looking
up those sites, http://www.wow.net/-harass/research.htm
and http://www.rhetorica.symposium.edu.uk/report.htm.
Mercy, didn't you see that there were links on most of the
names in http://www.rhetorica.symposium.edu.uk/report.
htm? The Hector McKerrow hyperlink took you to a New
Zealand university website, with a list of phone numbers
and addresses for all of the departments. The other names
were linked to other universities in England, Canada, Italy
and the US.

There was also a link on something called the 'Mahar
Foundation'. It looks like the Maher Foundation pays for
university people to get together and talk about things like
Quintilian's Institutes of Oratory.

If you ask me, the Hector McKerrow from http://
www.rhetorica.symposium.edu.uk/report.htm is a university professor from New Zealand, who's an expert on
Quintilian's Institutes of Oratory. I don't think he's the
guy you're looking for. My uncle's a university professor.
He spent his whole life studying to become one.

I checked out http:/www.wow.net/-harass/research.htm,

also. There were no hyperlinks. But I looked up Egon Kucyk, of the International Watchdog on Microwave Weapons, and he was on a couple of sites. He seems to have posted a letter that he wrote to a newspaper. And he was listed at the end of a web page belonging to someone called Stanley Hinsch.

Egon Kucyk's letter was hard to understand. He talked about clandestine bombardment with non-ionizing radiation, and how 'covert research into the modification of human brainwaves' should be made public. There was stuff about the human brain being a frequency receiver in the electromagnetic radiation spectrum and the scalar wave spectrum. I don't really know what he was talking about.

On his home page, Stanley Hinsch said that he was the victim of electronic surveillance, EEG cloning and playback harassment. There were about a million other pages, too, full of all this stuff about weak (1 mW) 4 Hz magnetic sine waves, and recognizing time relationships in the signal waveform – stuff that I couldn't understand. But it looks like he's pissed about something. He kept talking about gross human rights abuses, and that sounds bad.

I haven't gone through all of his site, yet. Even with a dictionary, it's hard to read.

Egon Kucyk is mentioned on the 'links' page. But the website given there doesn't exist any more.

Subject: Did you say that you were eleven
Sender: s.o.inoz – 12.14 p.m. February 21

Did you say that you were *eleven*, mousehound? You sound about fifty-three. I mean, what you've been doing – it's certainly impressive, but it's also kind of . . . well, creepy. What do you do all day, sit in front of a computer?

Subject: I spend a lot of time on my computer
Sender: mousehound – 9.43 p.m. February 20

I spend a lot of time on my computer. That's because I want to be a computer programmer when I grow up. I also want to design computer games. My father says it's a growth industry. He should know, because he's a bank manager. He lends money to companies that need to grow.

In New York, the winter is just as cold as it is in Nova Scotia. There's a lot of snow. But if you want to go tobogganing, or skating, there's always a hundred other people who want to do the same thing, and not enough space to do it in.

I'm not allowed out on my own, anyway, and my parents work long hours. Mostly, Rita (the nanny) looks after my brother Rupert, who's only three. He's no fun to play with, yet. We don't have a dog. Sometimes I go to the Museum of Natural History, to look at the dinosaurs, or to F.A.O. Schwarz, to look at the toys, but Rita always gets sore feet. And Rupert won't sit still in the Museum of Film and Television.

So yeah, I spend a lot of time on my computer. I don't see what's so creepy about that. It looks like you do, too.

Subject: As far as i'm concerned
Sender: keyop.1 – 10.53 a.m. February 21

As far as I'm concerned, you have your head screwed on tight, mousehound. The computer industry is an excellent career choice. I should know, because I'm in it myself. And it sounds to me as if you're exactly what my company is looking for.

I would suggest twenty points for your achievements so far. Would you like me to contact Ms Pryor's lawyers? They might feel happier speaking to an adult.

Subject: Hey come on be fair
Sender: zinglebrit – 9.13 a.m. February 21

Hey, come on. Be fair. Mercy should contact the lawyers. She's the one who wants to write Hector, after all. And if he decides to write back, then that can be her prize. Mousehound can have the clock radio.

Way to go, Mouse! (What *is* our real name?) Twenty points for you! And twenty for me, also, because guess what? I spoke to the director of *Cranks*, yesterday. He told me that, when Hector was making that movie, he lived with another actor called Perry Hentze in a rented house, right here in LA. And Perry Hentze is *still* in LA. So I'm gonna get in touch with his agent.

Oh, and it turns out that Hector's break in the 1980s wasn't because he couldn't get work. It was because he was sick. But Bob (that's the director's name, Bob) couldn't tell me what the trouble was. I guess it was probably what my dad calls 'Betty Ford-itis' – drugs or drink. Or both. Happens a lot, around here.

Subject: I'm going to write
Sender: mercynova – 3.40 p.m. February 21

I'm going to write to the lawyers. I'll enclose a letter for
Hector, and ask them to pass it on. Mousehound, can you
post their address? Please? Like Britt said, you can have
the clock radio. I just want to hear from Hector.

Subject: OK britt you're pretty clever
Sender: s.o.inoz – 7.10 a.m. February 22

OK, Britt, you're pretty clever, but check this out. I
borrowed one of my cousin's film reference books, on
Saturday, and looked up *Cranks*, and *Downside*, and *Last
Summer Blues*. I got a list of all the supporting actors in all
three films, and checked them out on the Internet. Do you
know that Gemma Frost was in *Last Summer Blues*? She
must have played a girlfriend, or something. I mean, I've
never even seen that show she's in now, but I knew there
was a good chance I'd find her on the Internet. And I did.
I found her fan club page.

The fan club page said that she would be interviewed on
some San Francisco radio station, live, at 10.30 p.m. on
Saturday evening, and that she would be taking questions.
When I worked out the time difference, I realized that
10.30 p.m. in San Francisco would be 5.30 p.m. yesterday
for me. So I called Directory Assistance and got the station
number and when I dialled it, they pretty much put me
straight through, probably because I was calling from
Australia. From what I could tell over the phone (because
they pipe the show through while you're waiting) all the

other callers were asking about the series she's doing, *First Line*, and David Ramone (yuk!), but I asked her what it was like, working with Hector McKerrow on *Last Summer Blues*, and if she knew what he was up to now.

Was she ever surprised by that question! And grateful too, I think – she must be sick of people asking about David Ramone and his cute little bum. She talked for a quite a long time. She said that she'd had a bit of a crush on Hector when they were making *Last Summer Blues*, but it was a one-way thing. Hector had been involved with somebody else, at the time. She said that he was very handsome, and very sweet, but also very moody. He could get very depressed, sometimes. Not that his moods ever interfered with his work. He was always punctual, always polite, always one hundred per cent committed. But when he was down, the work really took it out of him. He would get utterly exhausted, just from the effort of smiling and cracking jokes. And he wouldn't talk to anyone. He would sit behind his sunglasses, smoking or sleeping. She felt really sorry for him, then.

I think the announcer wanted her to get off the topic, at that stage, because how many people are interested in Hector McKerrow? So he asked her if she found her own work exhausting. But Gemma wouldn't be sidetracked. In fact, she was really great. I liked her. She was strong, and smart, and she had a cool sense of humour. Maybe I'll watch *First Line*, after all. On reflection, I think she'd play a pretty good hotshot defence lawyer.

Anyway, she went on to say that the last time she'd seen Hector had been four or five years ago, in a sports store, in a place called Albany, New York. Champs Sporting Goods. He was working there, in a run-down little mall.

She recognized him because of his eyes – she said they were still the same. He acted like he didn't want to talk to her, so she bought a few tennis balls and left.

She said she was glad that someone was still interested in his work. He'd been a great actor, with a lot of depth. Unfortunately, the announcer pretty much cut her off then. He actually *wanted* her to talk about David Ramone's bum.

So how's that for sleuth work, eh? Twenty points for me! And there's only one Champs sports store in Albany, so I managed to get the phone number. But the guy who answered said that he didn't know any Hector McKerrow.

I hope this clock radio is worth a big chunk of my birthday money. Because calls to the US aren't cheap.

Subject: Oh that's so sad
Sender: mercynova – 4.31 p.m. February 22

Oh, that's so sad. Working in a sports store! I've got to tell him how much I admire him. I've got to tell him that there are still people who love his work. Mousehound, where's that address?

Subject: Well done adamina
Sender: keyop.1 – 9.38 p.m. February 22

Well done, Adamina. Yes, twenty points for you. See? I told you that the world was a small place, these days. Twenty points for Britt, too. I must say, this site is becoming quite an addiction. I can't wait to see what happens next.

Subject: My name is aaron
Sender: mousehound – 8.00 p.m. February 22

My name is Aaron. The lawyers are called Piggot, Crane and Warning. Their address is Floor 12, 1203 Washington Street, Boston, Massachusetts.

Egon Kucyk's mailing address is in Albany, New York, but it's not a street number, it's a box number. The post office must hold his mail.

If Hector McKerrow used to work in Albany, then maybe he *is* the one who started that Free Thought Forum website. Maybe he and Egon Kucyk are friends. Maybe someone should send a letter to Egon Kucyk.

I don't want to. The websites are too strange. Stanley Hinsch is starting to look like a nut. I'm only on page twenty-three of sixty pages, but I think he thinks his brain is linked up to a satellite.

Subject: Thanks aaron
Sender: mercynova – 4.40 p.m. February 23

Thanks, Aaron. I'll write my letters tonight. Let's hope this works!

Subject: I see what you mean
Sender: s.o.inoz – 7.55 a.m. February 24

I see what you mean, Aaron. That Stanley Hinsch is a loony tune. I've been reading his manifesto (or whatever it is): 'Memory centres are being encrypted. Metal fillings are major targets. Surveillance zones are being created using electrical grids – brainwave monitoring no longer requires electrodes.' Bizarre.

I certainly hope Hector McKerrow *isn't* involved with him.

Subject: Hey y'all move over
Sender: dunkndive – 8.46 p.m. February 23

Hey, y'all, move OVER! I am ON the JOB! I live in Syracuse, I could SPIT and hit Albany, I'm gonna find Champs and I'm gonna FIND THIS DUDE! Make way for SLAM, ma friends! Make way for the BOSS! That clock is MINE! YOUR ASSES ARE MINE!

Subject: Did someone just fart
Sender: s.o.inoz – 3.10 p.m. February 24

Did someone just fart, on this message board?

Here's your update, Adamina – the latest from the Devlin house. Do you remember Sonny Johnson? He's that little blond boy from next door. Not Sandra's brother (Sandra's brother is a real jock called Chet), but the son of Shirley and Floyd. Floyd is a vague scientist who always puts his shirts on inside out, and forgets people's names. Shirley is a mean old busybody who hates the Devlins, but lets Sonny play with Troy because she wants to find out what's going on in the Devlin house. It's like she smells something fishy, but needs proof.

The joke's on her, though, because Sonny already knows about Troy being an alien. He found out in the very first episode. He thinks it's cool – he doesn't mind. And because Troy's his best friend, Sonny has promised not to tell anybody, not even his mom. That's why he's allowed to sleep over at the Devlins' house. (No one else is, much to Dixie's disappointment.) Sonny's even allowed to sleep in Troy's room, on Troy's bed, because Troy doesn't sleep in a bed. When he gets out of his boy suit, he slurps into a big vat, which is plugged into some kind of generator. Then he sits there, glowing all night, like molten steel, absorbing energy.

In the last episode, Sonny was sleeping over. He was very interested in Troy's boy suits. Troy has two suits, because every so often Sylvia has to clean one, and when that happens, Troy needs a spare. After trying on one of the suits – which made him look just like Troy – Sonny offered to take Troy's place on his Little League team. (I think they must be showing these episodes out of order, because last week people were playing football!) Troy loves baseball, but he's very bad at it. I guess running around in a boy suit makes him pretty uncoordinated. Sonny, however, is a terrific ball player. It soon became obvious that if Troy's lousy team was going to win its last game – instead of losing it, like every other game of the season – Troy was going to have to let Sonny impersonate him on the field.

That's what Sonny did, in the end. He went down to breakfast the next morning pretending to be Troy. Meanwhile, Troy slipped out of the house without anyone seeing him, slamming the front door, pretending to be Sonny heading back home. But of course he didn't go to Sonny's house. Instead he went off to the lake, where he practised his pitching for a while. In fact, he was chasing his baseball when he stumbled over Zac, who spends a lot of time by the lake, reading and watching girls. Zac was very surprised to see Troy. As far as he knew, Troy had driven off to Little League with Sylvia, that morning. But Troy explained what had happened, and Zac suggested a way of paying back 'the Jock Squad'. (He calls all these big, popular, athletic guys who hang out together 'the Jock Squad'.) You see, the night before, Zac had come out of a movie to find his beautiful motorbike covered with smashed eggs. So he had gone into the local high school hangout, which is called Ronnie's, to ask for water to clean the bike with. The Jock Squad was there, and one of them, Chet – Sandra's brother – made a joke about Zac being a rotten egg. Just the way he said it made Zac realize that the Jock Squad had egged his bike. That's why he wanted to pay them back.

His plan was pretty simple. While he went off to watch

Troy's team play baseball, under the watchful eye of its coach, Chet's father, Troy went back home. There he was able to sneak around without being noticed, because Sylvia was at the baseball game, Dixie was out shopping, and Dr Devlin was down in his basement lab, as usual. Using Zac's recipe, Troy mixed together a whole lot of chemicals and stuff and poured it into the gas tank of Chet's car, which was sitting out front of Sandra's house. Zac figured that, since he and Troy had perfect alibis, no one could ever accuse them of having anything to do with Chet's car – not even if Troy was seen. And he *was* seen, though not by Chet. He was seen by Floyd Johnson, who walked by without seeming to notice Troy.

By this time, Troy's team had won its last game, thanks to Sonny Johnson. He was the hero of the day. Despite all the cheering and back slapping, however, Sonny didn't want to hang around, because he was sick of impersonating Troy. When Zac offered to buy him a malted and take him to a movie (probably to extend their alibis), Sonny said that he wanted to go back home. But Sylvia liked the idea of Zac treating his brother. She made the two of them go off to Ronnie's diner for a malted, while she went home by herself.

Meanwhile, Troy was skulking in the garden, watching Chet trying to start his car. The car wouldn't start, though. In fact its entire engine fell on to the driveway, just as Floyd Johnson walked past, returning home from the grocery store. As Chet stomped about, screaming with rage, Floyd checked the damage. He said that some kind of acid must have been used.

Chet asked him if he'd seen anyone near the car. Floyd replied vaguely that he'd seen someone – it could have been Troy Devlin. So Chet stormed off to the Devlins' house, while Troy hid in a bush. Dr Devlin was the one who answered the door, and he told Chet that Troy was playing baseball. Then Chet's Dad arrived home with the whole baseball team, minus Sonny (alias Troy). Naturally, Chet wanted to know where Troy was. He discovered that Troy had last been seen heading for Ronnie's, with Zac, and ran off to punch them both out before explaining to his father what the problem was.

A few minutes later, Sylvia arrived home. She soon found Troy in the garden. Thinking that he must have given Zac the slip, she wouldn't listen to his protests, but threw him in the car and drove to Ronnie's. At Ronnie's, Zac and Sonny were sitting at a table next to Dixie and Sandra, talking to them. (At least, Zac was talking. Sonny was moping. He didn't want to be there. He didn't know what to say.) When Chet came in, and started shouting at the Devlins, Sandra defended them. She said that Zac and Troy had been at the baseball game all morning, so how could they have done anything to Chet's car? She said that Floyd Johnson was so vague, he never even knew what day it was.

Then Sylvia walked in with Troy.

It was a pretty tight spot for the Devlins! Of course, Sylvia instantly worked out what had happened. She very calmly told everyone that Troy had an identical twin, who was usually locked up in an insane asylum. Zac added that the insane twin must have trashed Chet's car, and Chet was so amazed that he just stood there, nodding.

As punishment, Zac and Troy had to pay Sylvia back, out of their weekly allowances, for having Chet's car repaired – because Dr Devlin wouldn't fix the car for them, and Chet wouldn't let Zac near his car, even though Zac offered to do the job himself.

Oh, and the dog this episode was quite placid except that it kept savagely attacking mailboxes. Just mailboxes – nothing else. So Sylvia had to pay for all the wiped-out mailboxes, also.

Subject: You know one of the things i totally love
Sender: zinglebrit – 4.00 p.m. February 24

You know one of the things I totally love about Hector McKerrow? That little, crooked canine tooth. It's so *cute*. Every set of teeth on TV now is so *ortho-perfect* – there's no charm, no individuality. When Hector smiles, my knees melt. And he doesn't do it often, does he? And his eyelashes are *so long*. I'm like, my *God*, this is *agony*.

Anyway, you'll be pleased to know that I've talked to Perry Hentze. I got his agent's number from the Screen Actors' Guild, and because my dad is my dad, the agent passed a message to Perry, who gave me a call. He seems like a nice guy. You might have seen him on *Walker, Texas Ranger*. Or *Silk Stalkings*. I haven't, but he told me that he gets a lot of work in small roles – like Hector used to. He told me that he read for the role Hector got in *Cranks*, and they met in the casting director's foyer, and then in a restaurant, and because Perry's lover had just thrown him out, and Hector was living in a hotel, they decided to rent a place together.

He said that they were roommates for nine months. He said that Hector was a total clean-freak, very tidy, very reliable, a terrific cook (with conservative tastes), quiet and unsociable (most of the time) but pleasant and polite to Perry's friends. He didn't drink much, but he smoked the odd joint, and when he did he would talk and talk and talk about the weirdest things. He also read some pretty weird books. I asked Perry what kind of things – what kind of books – but he couldn't really remember. Easter Island, he said. Magnetic fields. The Mafia. All kinds of stuff.

He said that Hector had trouble sleeping, and went running every day, and took good care of his health because he'd had a nervous breakdown. He wasn't just sick, guys, he was in hospital. For a long time. According to Perry, Hector was 'fragile'. Real sweet, he said, but delicate. Moody. Shy. You had to feel sorry for him. Forty-five years old, lovely voice, good looking, but as shy as a teenager. Perry tried to expand his social life, but Hector wouldn't play ball. He had a strange friend who would visit, and a girl, for a while, but no one else ever called except his agent, and his acting coach – business calls. I asked about the friend, and the girl, and Perry told me that the girl was an actress called Flo. Florence Kelloway. He said that one day, after she and Hector had had a knock-down, drag-out fight, Flo went off to Australia with an Australian actor called Tony Antonucci. I never heard of the guy, but maybe you have, Adamina? It's down to you, now. Maybe you can follow up on that lead.

As for the friend, his name was Gerry Modda. He was visiting from the East Coast, and slept on the couch for a week. Perry said that he was a slob, and spent most of his time watching the sports channel. When Gerry talked about his wife, Perry used to think 'Why the hell did she marry *this* guy?' It seemed like Gerry had come to Hector for advice, and they would mutter away for hours in Hector's bedroom. Hector said that Gerry (Perry and Gerry! Sounds like a comedy duo!) had had a hard time, but wouldn't say why. Perry thought that they must have met in the same nuthouse. He said that Gerry was a bit too excitable, but just laughed when I asked him why.

So, what kind of score would I get for this stuff? It's not post '91, but it's new information. Ten points? Fifteen points? I wish I could find a mug shot. Hector's agent can't help me. She threw out all of hers.

Subject: Thanks again
Sender: s.o.inoz – 3.50 p.m. February 25

Thanks again, Mercy. Your episode descriptions are very vivid. Britt, I've never heard of Florence Kelloway, but Tony Antonucci is a regular on one of our local TV shows, *The Heat*. It's about a bushfire brigade, and guess what? It's made by the same network that stupidly hired my cousin!

So I'll see what I can do.

Subject: Ten points for britt
Sender: keyop.1 – 12.05 p.m. February 25

Ten points for Britt, I think. Congratulations. And three points for me, because I've tracked down the elusive *Downside*. A friend of mine had it on tape. He's obsessed with Anna Guiterrez, you see, and she played a very small part as a prostitute in that film, before moving on to bigger and better things.

Hector wasn't the crook on the meat hook, Adamina. Oh, he *was* a crook – a drug dealer, to be specific – but he was decapitated on a speedboat. I think he brought a lot of style to that role. He was sleazy, but in a melancholy way. You could sense that the weight of his evil deeds was a burden too heavy for his mental equilibrium.

My quest now is to locate *Last Summer Blues*.

Subject: Is there any chance of you
Sender: mercynova – 4.02 p.m. February 25

Is there any chance of you copying *Downside* for me, Neville? Or any of the other movies that you find? I would really like to watch them.

Thanks again for all the other stuff about Hector.

Subject: Move over you guys
Sender: dunkndive – 6.16 p.m. February 25

MOVE OVER, you guys! Slam is back, and he is COOKIN. What's he up to now? He's plugged into a HOT Internet café, got a slice of pizza, got a coke, got the waitress in the palm of his hand – literally! – and he's in Hector's town, baby! Albany, NY! Been to Champs! Seen the guy there – name of Jerry. Jerry or Gerry? Jerry on the name tag. Gives me the *look*, you know? What the FU, right? Can't help me. Never hearda no Hector McKerrow. Greasy guy. Crater-face. Forties? Asks me, like, you gonna *buy* sumpin, punk? Thinks I'm gonna rip off the store, lift a coupla Reebox, whatever. So. What does Slam do? Goes to the drugstore opposite. Old girl's been there twelve years. She says, Hector Johnson? I say, Hector McKerrow. She says, Hector Johnson worked there in '95. 'Bout fifty. Real gentleman. Soft spoken. Handsome, but way too thin. Dressed like kinda grease monkey, dirty old pants, torn sweater, spark plug hangin on a cord around his neck. She says, Jerry hired the guy, far as I know. They worked together. She says, Jerry Modder. Em-oh-dee-dee-ee-err. M-o-d-d-e-r.

So I'm twenty, right? Twenty points. Don't tell me this Hector Johnson wasn't Hector McKerrow. Same time. Same town. Same first name. Same weirdo friend from the East Coast. Looks to me like Our Dude is BAD, man. False name? Gotta be an operator. And Jerry's in on it, too.

Jerry lives in a condo near the mall. I followed him there, after he shut the store, but it was goddam COLD out there, man, I nearly froze my ass off. So I came in here, it's open till two.

If Hector lives with Jerry, I'm gonna find out.

Subject: The case of j modder is mentioned
Sender: mousehound – 8.39 p.m. February 25

The case of J. Modder is mentioned in Stanley Hinsch's website. On page fifty-two he talks about J. Modder and R. Klein. J. Modder's 'activist background regarding government corruption has made him the subject of much overt intimidation including crank phone calls, intercepted mail, death threats, vandalism, break-ins'. R. Klein took part in an experiment, run 'covertly' by a 'major scientific body', in which microwaves were used to 'induce metabolic changes, alter brain functions, disrupt behaviour patterns, promote insomnia, and create memory loss'.

To sum up: a Hector McKerrow (of the Free Thought Forum) and an Egon Kucyk are both mentioned on Maynard Boyer's website. Egon Kucyk is also mentioned on Stanley Hinsch's website, along with J. Modder. J. Modder may have worked with Hector McKerrow (the actor) in Albany, NY, where Egon Kucyk has his postal address.

It seems like Hector McKerrow the actor and Hector McKerrow of the Free Thought Forum must be the same person.

I know it sounds stupid, but could all these people be plotting against the government?

Subject: I can't send you videotapes
Sender: keyop.1 – 12.55 p.m. February 26

I can't send you videotapes, Mercy – British VCRs and Canadian VCRs are incompatible.

Slam (or whatever your name is), I don't know what you think you're up to, but stalking people isn't the way to go about it. Don't you have anything better to do with your time? No points will be rewarded for any behaviour that amounts to harassment.

People have a right to their privacy, under the law.

Subject: This site is stupid
Sender: kewpet – 11.01 a.m. February 26

This site is stupid. Why are you all getting so hyped about some dumb actor?

Subject: He's not a dumb actor
Sender: mercynova – 4.30 p.m. February 26

He's not a dumb actor. If you knew what you were talking about, you wouldn't be saying that.

But maybe Neville's right. Maybe we should leave Hector alone.

Subject: Hey who do you think you are
Sender: dunkndive – 7.42 p.m. February 26

Hey! Who do you think you are, Neville No-dick? This isn't YOUR site, man, you're not the boss here, you didn't even start the damn thing, so YOU DON'T MAKE THE RULES! No one does! The web is FREE! And if you wanna talk about the law, I can tell you about the law, it SUCKS DICK. It's got a gun and an attitude and if you got no job, no money, no place to go, you can't turn around before you're up against the wall. I can't go to the drugstore for a Tylenol without some cop reams me because I'm not in school, didn't shave, got no job, and my shirt kicks ass. So I must be a dealer, right? Or a break-and-enter punk? Or whatever?

If I wanna come to Albany, visit my gramma, I can do

it, OK? It's supposed to be a free country. So be cool, take care of your own bizness, and let me take care of mine. Capeesh?

Subject: What did I tell you
Sender: s.o.inoz – 11.30 a.m. February 27

What did I tell you? The Internet is Loserville. Hey – let me ask you something, 'Slam'. (Or should I call you dunkndive? Or is it Duncan? I bet your real name's Duncan.) Have you ever laid eyes on Hector McKerrow? In anything? Or are you one of those sad people who jump on bandwagons without even asking themselves. 'Why the hell am I doing this?'

I've got to say that you sound like a drug dealer in a very, very C-grade movie starring Chuck Norris.

You'll all be pleased to know that I gave my cousin a letter for Tony Antonucci. He's passed it on to one of the guys who does sound editing on *The Heat*, and that guy's going to pass it on to the director, who's going to pass it on to Tony.

So let's hope he gets it.

Subject: Hey let's all chill out
Sender: zinglebrit – 7.30 p.m. February 26

Hey, let's all chill out, here, OK? Let's not forget that we're all meant to be *united* in our love for Hector and his dreamy eyes and his cute little canine tooth.

I drove past the house that Hector was renting in '91,

today. It's the color of mustard, and really small. From the condition of the blinds, I'd say that it was still being rented.

I felt like a tourist in Beverly Hills.

Subject: I think you'll find
Sender: keyop.1. – 12.59 p.m. February 27

I think you'll find, Slam, that the Italians spell it 'capisi'. Not capeesh. But then I don't suppose you actually finished high school.

Subject: This is a question for dunkndive
Sender: mousehound – 3.22 p.m. February 27

This is a question for dunkndive. You said that Hector Johnson was wearing a spark plug around his neck, when he worked at Champs. Was it really a spark plug, or did it just look like a spark plug? Did you get any more information about it? Because Stanley Hinsch has a list of links on his website, and one of them is Mind Body/Research (http://www.thebook.com/mindbody/research.html). It's the site for something called the Institute of Technical Energy Medicine (ITEM), in Moscow. ITEM uses something called an aura and brain imaging system, where they map out the 'bioenergies' of people's brains. It's kind of hard to understand, but I guess it's meant to be healthy. They also sell things. They sell the Novoton Biocorrector, which has a whole page to itself. The Novoton Biocorrector is supposed to reduce pain, improve concentration, promote relaxation, and stop you from feeling tired. It's 'a high technology defence against harmful subtle energies, electromagnetic radiation, geopathic radiation zones, and harmful psychic information energy'. You can buy it for $45, plus $3 shipping and handling.

If you check out the ITEM website, you'll see a picture of the Novoton Biocorrector. It looks a bit like a spark plug, or a piece of electrical equipment. Not very big. You wear it around your neck, on a cord.

Dunkndive, I think you should download that picture, get a printout, and take it to the lady in the drugstore.

Subject: I don't understand
Sender: mercynova – 5.58 p.m. February 27

I don't understand. What do you think it all means, Aaron? Do you think Hector's sick? Is that what you mean?

I've checked out that website, and I don't think what they do is a *bad* thing. The way they talk, it's like aroma-therapy, or acupuncture. Isn't it?

Subject: Got it hound–dog way to go
Sender: dunkndive – 8.11 p.m. February 27

Got it, hound-dog. Way to go, man. I got the shot – this Novoton Biocorrector looks like a piece of computer, right? The print quality's shit on the machine they got here, but it's good enough. I'll take it to the drugstore Monday. (Sundays it's closed, would you believe?)

HEY – NEVILLE! KISS MY ASS, OK? And you, too, you dog-faced Ozzi bitch. Sure, my name's Duncan – what's it to you? Better than Adamina. Adamina sounds like a laxative.

I've been hanging around Jerry's condo, and I'm pretty sure he's livin alone. No one else goes in or out. Twice he made calls from a payphone on the corner. TWICE. Like he can't use his mobile? Like hell. And you know why he made the second call? Because I went to his apartment. Pushed the intercom. (No doorman.) Guy says, 'Who is it?' I say, 'Hector?', even though I recognize the voice. He says, 'Who is this?' I say, 'Jerry?' He says, 'Yeah, who are you?' I say, 'Frienda Hector's, man.' He says, 'Wrong address, pal.' He won't talk to me again. I push the button a coupla more times, but no joy. So I wait behind a bus shelter, and sure enough he comes out after about an hour. Goes to the payphone. I follow him. While he's talkin, I come up behind – there's no door on the booth. I hear him say 'Could be', then 'I dunno.' Then he sees me. 'Whadayou want?' I hold up a quarter. He says, 'You wanna gimme a little space here, pal? Uh?' So I give him the finger, he hangs up, calls me a punk and walks away.

Know what I think? I think that was Hector on the line. Or whoever bumped off Hector. But Jerry knows my face, now, so I gotta watch my back.

I can't stay here much longer. Gramma don't want me, and there's no action goin down. It's worse than Syracuse. At least there I KNOW people. And I miss my computer. These cafés stink – they rip you off, man, like four bucks for a goddam coffee.

Subject: Slam you are going to find
Sender: keyop.1 – 9.04 a.m. February 28

Slam, you are going to find yourself in big trouble, my friend. You'll be up for loitering with intent, and the proof is all here, in black and white. You won't score any points by these means. They won't be awarded. I suggest you return to Syracuse as soon as possible.

I refuse to be implicated in anything of this nature.

Subject: Ok everyone hold on to your hats
Sender: s.o.inoz – 9.35 p.m. February 28

OK, everyone. Hold on to your hats. This here is worth a good twenty points, *at least*, and I didn't stalk anyone to get it.

Tony Antonucci phoned today. He'd read my letter, and sounded perfectly normal, which surprised me; on TV he comes off like something squeezed out of a tube. Anyway, he told me that Florence Kelloway went back to America six years ago. He and she were both dead broke, at the time, and fighting a lot – *about Hector McKerrow*, among other things. You see, Hector came out here in 1994. Yes, that's right – to Australia. (God, I could have met him!) Florence had told Tony a few choice things about her weird ex, including the fact that he used to spy on her, and go through her purse, and talk to the TV, so Tony wasn't too thrilled when he turned up on the doorstep. Especially since Tony was very young, then, and Hector was pushing fifty. But he said that Hector seemed OK, at first; a good guest, much neater than his hosts, always up before they were, with the sofa bed folded away and the coffee made and the cat fed. After a couple of days, though, Tony began to get jealous. He said (and this shows you what a nice, normal guy he is) he said that Hector was a *presence*, that he himself wasn't a bad actor, he'd done a few good things, he had a good technique and a look that worked, but Hector was something else. Like Brando, maybe. Really tormented and smouldering under the 'noble ruins' of this beautiful face. Haunted eyes. Very fluid. Terrific diction, though he was quite soft-spoken and his training had been patchy. A natural, is what Tony said. Anyway, though it became increasingly obvious that Hector was (as Tony put it) one can short of a six-pack, he was also fascinating and compelling and he began to dominate the whole 'scene'. After three days, Florence was hanging on to his every word and discussing him obsessively when he wasn't around, which didn't happen often, because he had major jet lag. *Major* jet lag. He spent most of the first day lying on the lounge with his eyes shut.

Tony said that after five days, he'd had enough. He couldn't live under the constant surveillance of Hector, whose every glance was invested with layers and layers of the most tortured meaning, though he never said much. Also, he was travelling under an assumed name – Johnson. (He told Flo that he'd changed it.) Also, Hector was an insomniac, and had the TV on all the time, and wouldn't meet Tony's friends, and skulked around outdoors in sunglasses and a hat pulled down over his hair, which was distinctive, according to Tony, very thick and silvery. Tony asked him straight out if he was on the run, or something, but Hector said no. Then Flo and Tony had a big fight about him, and Hector left. Flo said he'd gone to

Tasmania. A couple of weeks later she met with him in a café, and Tony was furious, and he and Flo had another big fight, and she moved out for a month.

Tony told me that he and Flo could never agree about anything. But he was sorry, now, that he hadn't let Hector stick around, because he was such an interesting person, such a romantic figure, spooky but attractive, and far more deserving of attention than Florence. Florence, he said, is completely obsessed with her own image. Everything – her clothes, her friends, her bedroom, the story of her life – has to conform with her ideals of perfection. According to Tony, she's a childish little cow.

Nevertheless, he gave me her address in Toronto, Canada. (She moved there two years ago.) So I rang Directory Assistance, and got her number, and rang it, and guess what? She was in! I told her about this message board, and she thought it was really funny. She said that if she knew where Hector was, she'd go for the clock radio herself, but she doesn't.

The last she saw of him was right here, in Sydney, when he came back from Tasmania. He called her from a dump of a hotel in Kings Cross, and they met at a café on Darlinghurst Road. He was very unhappy. He'd been to Strahan, which is this tiny little town in western Tasmania, but he hadn't found what he was looking for, there. When I asked Florence what he was looking for, she said: 'Who knows? Sanctuary, maybe. He was always running away from things.' Then, when I said, 'What things?', she said, 'Himself.'

According to Florence, Hector was in hospital for schizophrenia from 1988 to 1990. Florence was only twenty-three when they got together, so she reckons she was too young to understand what that might mean in a relationship. What it meant, apparently, was that Hector was insanely jealous, questioning her about her movements, following her when she went out, preventing her from using the phone, hiding her car keys. It also meant that he would 'tune out' for hours, not even hearing when she spoke to him. 'I guess I was the one who came on to him,' she said, 'because he was attractive, really attractive for an older guy, like a lot of male actors; they get sexier as they get older. But I should have known. A guy that age, drifting about, no property, no partner . . . he had to have problems. And he did. He just wouldn't face up to himself. Wouldn't admit that he was sick.'

Florence said that she was practically driven into the arms of another man – not Tony, but some guy she saw for a few weeks before she met Tony, a guy called Ivan. Hector found out about that, and threw her against a wall. So she left. For weeks afterwards, she told me, Ivan would call her, complaining that Hector was stalking him, hanging around his apartment block, following him to work.

I would have liked to talk more, but I couldn't afford it. I wanted to ask her what Hector was really *like*, you know? I mean, he couldn't have been all *that* crazy, or why would people always have found him so attractive? Florence told me he had charm, but what does that mean? She told me he had a beautiful smile, and that he cooked for her. She also said that she must have been looking for a substitute father, because he was twice her age.

I had to cut her off, then, before she told me all about her personal problems, and how her father had abandoned her mother when she was three.

So. Beat that, *Slam*. I wish I knew what Hector was doing in Tasmania. Why Tasmania, of all places? Though if he was running away from something – or someone – he couldn't have run any farther than Strahan. I've been there. It's very isolated, though it's become a bit of a tourist destination (which is why we went). Lots of mist and rain and endless forest. Spooky.

It kills me to say so, but I think that our friend Slam might be right. It's beginning to look a little suss, isn't it?

Poor Hector.

Subject: Oh my this is so sad
Sender: mercynova – 1.32 p.m. February 28

Oh my, this is so sad. I can't bear it that Hector's turned out like this. I don't want to think of him as old, and sick, and running away. Maybe I shouldn't have started this message board.

Subject: Is that how you feel
Sender: zinglebrit – 1.01 p.m. February 28

Is that how you feel? Mercy, I'm like, how sexy can one man *get*? Brooding, possessive, 'every glance invested with layers and layers of the most tortured meaning', my *God*. Let me *at* him. And he's still got all his hair! Sean Connery hasn't. My dad's fifty-nine, and he's as bald as a billiard ball.

You write really well, Adamina. I could see everything like it was a movie. Do you think there's anyone in

Tasmania who might know more? (It's in the same country, right? I mean, Tasmania is part of Australia, isn't it? I can't really tell, from my atlas.)

Subject: Britt is right adamina
Sender: keyop.1 – 10.45 p.m. February 28

Britt is right, Adamina. You ought to think about becoming a journalist. Your style is very clean, and it's not everyone who can wheedle information out of people over the telephone. Twenty points for you.

Is anybody keeping track of these totals?

Subject: Hey man who says you get to chalk
Sender: dunkndive – 8.07 p.m. February 28

Hey, man, who says you get to chalk up the scores? What makes YOU the man? I say we VOTE on it. Twenty points for the Ozzi? All those in favor, say 'I'. (She gets my vote. She might be a pain in the ass, but her stuff is good stuff.)

Subject: A journalist no thanks
Sender: s.o.inoz – 3.58 p.m. March 1

A journalist? No *thanks*. The media is about as low as you can get, as far as I'm concerned. Vultures and parasites. The last thing I want to be is someone who runs around interviewing the parents of murder victims. Besides, I don't much like talking to people. I liked reading in my room.

I might be a pain in the ass, Slam, but at least I know how to spell 'aye'. Unlike some others on this message board.

Subject: This is a great board
Sender: tinkerball – 10.02 a.m. March 1

This is a great board. I'm really enjoying it. But Slam is gross and Adamina should be more positive about things.

Subject: A letter just arrived
Sender: mercynova – 4.13 p.m. March 1

A letter just arrived from Piggot, Crane and Warning. It says that Ms Pryor's alimony used to be paid from an account, regularly, but that this account was closed several years ago. Now the money arrives in cash, at their office, in a sealed envelope, which they forward to Ms Pryor. Since the envelope bears no return address, they have no idea where Mr McKerrow is now residing. He no longer retains the services of his former lawyer, his former theatrical agent, or his former bank. They would very much like to know where he might be found, but unless he stops meeting his financial obligations, they cannot feel justified in the expense of pursuing him.

I think maybe they're hoping that we might find him ourselves.

Subject: What about the postmark
Sender: zinglebrit – 1.31 p.m. March 1

What about the postmark? Mercy, ask them about the postmark on the envelope with the money in it!

Subject: I just talked to patty pryor
Sender: mousehound – 8.09 p.m. March 1

I just talked to Patty Pryor. I told her what the lawyers said, and she told me that the envelope of money they send her, which is enclosed inside another envelope, has Hector's writing on it, but no postmark. So he must drop it at the lawyers' office himself – or someone else must.

That might mean he's living in Boston.

Subject: I honestly think that this has gone far enough
Sender: keyop.1 – 8.15 a.m. March 2

I honestly think that this has gone far enough. People, this is harassment. And no points are awarded for harassment.

Subject: Hey butt out
Sender: dunkndive – 9.41 a.m. March 1

Hey! But out, Neville! Twenty points for Aaron – who wants to argue?

Subject: No argument from me
Sender: zinglebrit – 12.44 p.m. March 2

No argument from me. My sister goes to college in Cambridge, Mass (M.I.T., as a matter of fact!). Pity I can't ask her to stake out the lawyers' office. Pity I can't go stay with her, and do it myself. What about you, Slam? Syracuse is closer to Boston than LA.

Hey – when's the next alimony payment due?

Subject: Great board
Sender: waddiex – 2.16 p.m. March 2

Great board. Someone just told me about it. A friend of mine once met Hector McKerrow at a party, back in the eighties. It was at a beach house, and some girl died of an overdose. Hector was wandering about at sunrise, and he found her with a guy – they'd been partying all night on the dunes. The guy was stoned off his head, like, comatose. The girl was naked.

Hector put all her clothes back on her before he went and called the paramedics. My friend heard the cops giving him shit about that – disturbing the evidence – but Hector had a great attitude. He told 'em that if they wanted shots of naked girls, they should subscribe to *Playboy*. He said he was preserving her dignity.

What kind of points do I get for this?

Subject: Ten points for waddiex
Sender: dunkndive – 5.38 p.m. March 2

Ten points for waddiex – unless someone's got a problem with my math. Britt, I'm unemployed, OK? My dad was a welder, till he got shafted. My mom works at a laundro-mat. Whaddaya think, I got money to burn?

You got the money. You got the sister. Go check the place out. Get DOWN, baby!

Mousehound, my man, I gave old Mrs Drugstore an eyeful of your spark plug, today, and she said it looks like the same one as Hector's, but she's real old and her memory's not so good. Do you think this Moscow crew has some kinda customer database? I dunno – I'm no hacker, but you sound like one. Maybe you could check it out.

Subject: Slam i'd like to help
Sender: zinglebrit – 5.03 p.m. March 2

Slam, I'd like to help. Really. But my money's in trust, I happen to be at school, right now, and I can't stake out the lawyers' office because it's tricky, in a wheelchair. If I sat on a street corner all day, people would start throwing quarters at me.

So please. This isn't an episode of *Ironside*.

Subject: But britt you said you played basketball
Sender: mercynova – 8.45 p.m. March 2

But Britt, you said you played basketball. How can you be in a wheelchair?

Subject: I'm sorry britt
Sender: s.o.inoz – 12.59 p.m. March 3

I'm sorry, Britt, I'm so sorry. You should have told us.

Subject: I saw hector mckerrow
Sender: croozer – 11.00 p.m. March 2

I saw Hector McKerrow today. He was drinking in a bar. He was in Madrid, Spain.

Last night's episode started with a bang – Zac in hospital! Don't worry, though. He only broke his arm, falling off his bike. He was very embarrassed about it. And he was *very* worried about his bike. When Sylvia came to pick him up from the hospital, she met Sandra's mother Mavis, who was selling flowers and candy in the little shop run by volunteers from some kind of hospital ladies' committee. Mavis, I should tell you, is sweet and shy, and always nice to everyone, though she was obviously a little scared of Sylvia. (*Everyone* is a little scared of Sylvia.) They talked about the ladies' committee, and Sylvia said she wanted to become a member. So Mavis told her to come along to the meeting, that night.

But it turned out that mean old Shirley Johnson was the president of the hospital ladies' committee. She was horrified when Sylvia showed up. So were most of the other ladies. When they started to plan the next volunteer roster, they wouldn't let Sylvia work in the shop, or push a trolley around the wards, or even serve at the bake sale they were planning. At last, however, they agreed that she could make cookies for the sale.

Well, she sure made some cookies! She baked all day and all night (because she doesn't sleep, of course) until the house was full of them, and she had to rent a truck to deliver them to the local church hall. Meanwhile, the Devlins' new dog was making a big mess of things, because it was a burrowing dog, and had disappeared underground. It was digging holes and tunnels all over the yard, toppling shrubs and destroying flowerbeds. Even Troy couldn't catch it, though he spent a lot of time with fishing rods and dog biscuits and flashlights, trying to track it down.

As for Dixie, that poor girl had tried to dye her hair red, because Chet's new girlfriend was a red-head (Dixie's totally stuck on Chet), and something had gone terribly wrong. Her hair had turned green. The day of the bake sale, she wouldn't leave her room, not even with a scarf tied over her head. Zac wouldn't go out, either – he didn't want people asking him how he broke his arm. Dr Devlin was away, and Troy was busy chasing the dog. So Sylvia delivered her cookies to the bake sale all by herself, then returned the truck and went off to her quilting class.

Back at the Devlins' house, Sandra – who had heard from her mother that Zac's arm was broken – dropped by with some cookies of her own. Dixie had cancelled on her the night before, saying that she was sick, and Sandra wanted to pay her a visit, too. But Dixie didn't want anyone seeing her hair until it had been fixed by a professional hairdresser. Unfortunately, the local hairdresser was fully booked until the next day. (All the kids were on vacation, by the way, because Zac had complained about the accident ruining his summer break.) Zac tried to stop Sandra from going up to Dixie's room by telling all kinds of funny lies about how sick she was, until Sandra got quite frightened. Anyway, it was Troy who spilled the beans, at last. He came into the house, saying that he was tired of chasing the dog, and mentioned Dixie's hair.

Of course, Sandra didn't laugh at poor Dixie. Sandra was too nice. Instead, she offered to fix Dixie's hair herself, by dyeing it black, and that's exactly what she did. In the meantime, because Dixie had chewed him out, Troy left the house in a huff. He met up with Sonny Johnson, who went with him to play baseball in the park behind the church hall. Here, they saw all of Sylvia's cookies put out with the garbage (even though the bake sale was still on), and Sonny just couldn't resist them. Troy doesn't eat food, unless he absolutely has to, but Sonny ate and ate until he started feeling sick. So he went home, and Troy went home, and Troy told Zac about the cookies. Boy, was Zac mad! He loves his mother, and he hates it when people are cruel to her.

Then Shirley Johnson turned up at the house, saying that Sonny had food poisoning from Sylvia's cookies, and that Sylvia shouldn't be allowed to handle food. She wanted to talk to Sylvia or Dr Devlin, but Zac told her that they weren't home. He told her that Sonny was puking his guts out because he was a pig, and accused her of throwing all Sylvia's cookies away. Three cheers for Zac! He was terrific. He knew how to stand up to Shirley Johnson. She got all flustered, but when she walked out of the house, instead of going home, she went creeping around to the basement window, to have a peek inside. She knew that Troy and Dixie were upstairs, you see, and that Sylvia and Dr Devlin were away.

What she didn't know was that the Devlins' yard wasn't safe any more. She fell down one of the dog's freshly dug holes, and broke her ankle. Needless to say, it was Sylvia who took her place in the hospital shop for two weeks, or whatever, and who cooked a beautiful meal for Shirley's guests that evening — because Shirley's husband's boss was invited for dinner, and Shirley didn't want to cancel.

You'll also be pleased to know that Dixie's hair turned

out just fine. It made her look very French and sexy, and Chet was hugely impressed. As for the dog, it burrowed out of the Devlins' garden, and was never seen again.

Croozer, are you absolutely sure you saw Hector in Spain? Spain is a long way from Boston – unless Piggott, Crane and Warning have offices in Madrid, too.

Subject: Yeah that's right croozer
Sender: s.o.inoz – 8.22 a.m. March 4

Yeah. That's right, croozer. We want more details. Who are you, and how come you recognized Hector McKerrow? No points without proof.

Oh – thanks for the rundown, Mercy. Sounds like it was a good episode.

Subject: I'm not a hacker
Sender: mousehound – 6.16 p.m. March 3

I'm not a hacker, Slam. Even if the Institute of Technical Energy Medicine had a customer database, I couldn't tap into it. I wouldn't know how. Anyway, isn't it illegal?

I taped *The Family Way*, last night, I didn't think Zac was so great. In fact, I thought the whole thing was kind of stupid. But I did like the dog.

76

Subject: The family way is sinful and wrong
Sender: witness++! – 6.14 p.m. March 3

The Family Way is sinful and wrong. It's the Devil's work. You should all turn away from sin, and filth like this. The Bible says, 'Lift up your eyes and behold.' Don't condemn yourselves by watching this depraved show.

Subject: Oh puhlease now we get the crazies
Sender: zinglebrit – 6.35 p.m. March 3

Oh, puh*lease*. Now we get the crazies. Like, I'm sure *The Family Way* is really going to mess with our minds, right?

Great episode, by the way. I loved Zac's jammies – very cute. Croozer, if we don't hear from you soon, we'll know you're lying. No one's getting my clock radio without a convincing story. Like Adamina said – no points without proof. You got an autographed beer mat, or something?

Paraplegics *can* play basketball, Mercy. When we set our minds to it.

Subject: I was surfing the net for
Sender: quarxor – 10.20 p.m. March 3

I was surfing the net for Gemma Frost references (because I'm a big fan) and look what I found! The Mystery of the Missing Psycho. Listen, I'm an M.I.T. sophomore. I live in Boston's North End. It wouldn't take me long to get to Washington Street. I could stake out those lawyers any time – just tell me when Hector usually makes the drop. I'll look out for a grease monkey with silver hair. (Can somebody *please* post a picture?)

Subject: Well here i am back in syracuse
Sender: dunkndive – 11.11 p.m. March 3

Well, here I am, back in Syracuse. My gramma kicked me out. But that's OK, because I went through Jerry's trash before I left (GODDAM, I nearly puked!) and found a torn-up phone bill, all covered in pizza and coffee grounds. (Let's get this straight, OK? It's FIFTY POINTS for trash.) Anyhow, I stuck the pieces together, they're here in fronta me, and whaddaya know? Jerry made three calls to Boston last month. Same number every time, but not the lawyers – some girl. I got her answering machine. 'Hi, you've called Stephanie. I'm not here right now, so please leave your name and number after the tone.' I told her to get her ass in gear, left my number, called Directory Assistance, but they wouldn't give me squat. No address, no nuthin. Old Steph's got a silent number, which means they won't give me the time of day.

So. Anyone wanna help me, here? The number's 617 893 3111. Aaron, man, you GOTTA know how to hack into the phone system. People do it ALL THE TIME. Or maybe Mr M.I.T. can do it, since he's so smart. Hey, what are the odds that Hector's holed up with Stephanie? If he is, he could drop off Patty's cash any time.

Looks like I'm gonna win that radio.

Subject: This has gone far enough
Sender: keyop.1 – 12.15 p.m. March 4

This had gone far enough. I mean it. Sifting through garbage is beyond a joke, but publishing silent phone numbers *must* be illegal. My collection of Hector McKerrow memorabilia is no longer on offer; I will not be awarding any more points. Please will everyone desist? Your quarry does not deserve this kind of intrusion. It's wrong.

What's more, it probably won't get you anywhere. That message from 'croozer' was a hoax. Allegedly, he saw Hector McKerrow in Madrid, Spain, on March 2. But he logged on at 11.00 p.m. that night, which means that he couldn't have been in Spain at all. Why? Because Adamina logged on just before him, at 12.59 p.m. on March 3. It's a matter of time zones. If croozer had truly been in Madrid, he would have logged on after 2 a.m. on March 2. At a guess, I'd say that croozer logged on somewhere along the east coast of Canada, or the US.

People, it's easy to lie on the Internet. For all we know, Slam might have concocted the whole Albany episode. For all *you* know, I might be the police! Let's reconsider, shall we? Mercy, it's your call. This is your message board. Do you really want to torment the poor man like this?

Subject: Maybe neville's right
Sender: mercynova – 4.39 p.m. March 4

Maybe Neville's right. Maybe we should stop. Slam, you shouldn't be going through people's garbage. This isn't what I wanted. If Hector doesn't want to talk, maybe we should leave him alone.

Maybe I should close this message board.

Subject: I told you i'm not a hacker
Sender: mousehound – 6.40 p.m. March 4

I told you I'm not a hacker, Slam. I can't get into the phone system, even if I wanted to, which I don't. You can get prosecuted for that.

Patty Pryor's alimony arrives around the middle of the month. She told me it has to be paid to the lawyers by the fifteenth.

If you close this message board, Mercy, it'll be easy enough to start another one.

Subject: Yeah that's right
Sender: dunkndive – 8.03 p.m. March 4

Yeah! That's right! You tell 'em, Mouse! I'LL start a new one; no tight-ass English chickenshits allowed! Kiss my butt, Neville! Hey, where's that M.I.T. computer weener? C'mon, man, I asked you a question!

Left another message on Steph's answering machine.

Subject: It's 'wiener' dickwad
Sender: quarxor – 11.04 p.m. March 4

It's 'wiener', dickwad, not 'weener'. And I'm no computer whiz; I happen to be studying architecture. We're not *all* silicon geeks at M.I.T., you know. Though I could probably dig up a few, if necessary.

Luckily, you don't have to be Bill Gates when it comes to technology like answering machines. I called Stephanie's number, and there was a handful of messages. What's more, the beeps sounded familiar. So I took a chance, and ba-boom! She's got the same kind of answering machine as I have. Prewar, you know? Antique. A one-digit retrieval code, and I got it first try.

Message number one was from a charity. They called her 'Ms Stephanie Homenko'. Message number two was from a friend. She plays squash. Message number three was from Duncan, so we can ignore it. Message number four was from 'David', and was X-rated; it's obvious that they're an item. Message number five was from a colleague – gossip from work. A bank was mentioned (it's classified), so I called the bank switchboard, and asked to be put through to Stephanie Homenko. They put me through to a particular branch in a particular street in Boston – and sorry, guys, it's privileged information! I'll release it after I have first shot.

What do you think it's worth, this stuff? I think about ten points for initiative, myself.

Subject: My brother goes to school with britt
Sender: barnuts – 9.27 p.m. March 4

My brother goes to school with Britt, which is how I heard about this site. I was talking to my mom's new boyfriend, yesterday, and he said that Hector McKerrow once threw a bowl of guacamole at a friend of his. He said it happened twenty years ago, at a dinner party.

How many points would I get for this?

Subject: No more points
Sender: keyop.1 – 12.55 p.m. March 5

No more points. The competition is *over*. Britt, if you withdraw your clock radio, there won't be anything left to win. Please. Hector McKerrow has a right to his privacy – as, I might say, does Stephanie Homenko.

Subject: I dunno neville
Sender: zinglebrit – 1.04 p.m. March 5

I dunno, Neville. I'm like, *does* Hector have a right to his privacy? Supposing he's a drug dealer? Supposing he's on the run from the law? Don't you think it's pretty *weird*, the way he's changed his name? The way he pays his alimony in cash? The way he's been wearing gadgets from Moscow?

I mean, what if we're doing the right thing, here? What if he's committed a crime, and we track him down?

Barnuts, you've got to be Gabby Liebermann. I've told

my friend Felicia about this site, and Felicia's going out with Malachi Liebermann, who's *got* to be your brother. Unless you're Darilyn Paul? I've told Glenn Paul about this site. Oh – and Martin Lourenco, too.

As a matter of fact, now I think about it, I've told a lot of people.

Subject: Do you really think hector's a criminal
Sender: mercynova – 4.49 p.m. March 5

Do you really think Hector's a criminal, Britt? Gee, I hope not. What if he is? What if he gets real mad? Slam, you'd better be careful. Maybe we should stop this right now.

Subject: Are you kidding
Sender: dunkndive – 7.13 p.m. March 5

Are you kidding? If Hector's crooked, we GOTTA stop him! Take him OUT. Hey, M.I.T. man, your shit ain't worth ten points, no way! So you've tracked down Stephanie. So what? If she's shacked up with Hector, THAT'S worth points. If she's his courier, THAT'S worth points. So far, waddawe got on her? Zilch. OK, so Jerry Modder calls her sometimes. So what? You find a connection, you get the points. And what's this 'privileged information' garbage? You work for the Defense Department, or what? This is FREE SPACE, man! This is ONLINE DEMOCRACY. What we got, we share!

Barnuts, you can have three points for the effort.

Subject: You're not the ultimate authority
Sender: quarxor – 10.19 p.m. March 5

You're not the ultimate authority here, Duncan. When it comes to points scores, we're supposed to be voting, remember? I vote five points for barnuts, ten points for me. And another ten on top of that, because I stopped by Stephanie's bank today and looked for the lady with the 'Stephanie' name tag. She's about thirty, thin, blonde, nothing special. There are two kinds of bank tellers – bubbly and sulky. She's sulky. She's doesn't wear a wedding ring.

I wanted to follow her home when the branch closed, but she must have left by the back door. So it'll have to be Monday.

Subject: I agree with slam
Sender: lerger – 8.17 p.m. March 5

I agree with Slam. That M.I.T. guy doesn't deserve any points. Not yet, anyway.

This board is the *best*.

Subject: Keyop.1 are you neville pratt
Sender: mousehound – 11.28 a.m. March 6

Keyop.1, are you Neville Pratt?

I was just reading about Neville Pratt in *Web Guide* magazine. He's an English millionaire, forty-four, who's the founder and managing director of Unus. Unus is one of

Britain's biggest Net service providers. Neville Pratt wears glasses, and spends a lot of time on the Net. He has a Rolls-Royce and a Mercedes, and lives in a big house in the country.

I'm only asking if you're the same guy because your e-mail address is prattboss@unus.com.uk. Also, I wondered if keyop.1 stands for keyboard operator number one. Kind of a joke, or something?

If you *are* Neville Pratt, then maybe you can tell me which is the best search engine, because it seems to me that Alta Vista and Yahoo! sometimes cover totally different ground, you know what I mean?

I think Slam is right about quarxor's point score, but not about barnuts'. I think barnuts deserves a five.

Subject: Oooh baby
Sender: dunkndive – 3.00 p.m. March 6

Oooh, baby! So Neville's loaded, is he? Figures. Thinks he's such a big shot. Well, not on this site!

I talked to Stephanie Homenko, today. Called her up and she answered. IN PERSON. 'Yup,' she says, 'this is Stephanie.' I say, 'Jerry Modder's friend?' she says, 'Yes. I know Jerry. Who's this?' I say, 'This is Duncan.' 'Who?' 'Duncan. Is Hector there?' she says, 'I don't know any Duncan.' I say, 'It's important, OK? I gotta speak to Hector.' Then she hung up.

I tried a second time, but when she heard my voice, she hung up again. The third time, she said to me, 'Get off this line, or I'll call the police.' I thought, SURE you will, baby. Sure you will. But I didn't push it.

So – no joy there.

Subject: This is so cool
Sender: zinglebrit – 3.30 p.m. March 6

This is so cool. Neville, why didn't you tell us? A millionaire computer geek! (I'll have to get a copy of *Web Guide*.) Hey, if you're really a super-nerd, then can't you hack into Social Security or the Police Department, or something, and find out Hector McKerrow's address?

Subject: I'm another australian
Sender: hoggetty – 10.00 a.m. March 7

I'm another Australian, and I live in Strahan. That's how I found this message board – surfing for Strahan sites. It's not the end of the world here, you know. We do have the Internet – and we also have fascinating river cruises, trout breeding, beautiful objects made from the unique Huon pine, quaint holiday cottages, convict ruins, and kilometres of deserted beach.

If you come to Tasmania, don't forget to visit! We'd love to meet you.

Subject: Whether i'm neville pratt or not
Sender: keyop.1 – 11.00 p.m. March 6

Whether I'm Neville Pratt or not is no concern of yours, Aaron. We use handles on these sites to preserve our anonymity. As I said before, it's easy to lie on the Internet.

For all you know, I could be anyone. Hell, I could be Hector McKerrow!

Subject: You're not hector mckerrow
Sender: mercynova – 12.02 p.m. March 7

You're not Hector McKerrow, are you? Or are you? The stuff you sent me had English stamps on it, but . . . I guess Hector *could* be living in England.

If you really are Hector, Neville, then you already know how I feel about you. I think you were great in *The Family Way*, and in *Cranks*. (I saw *Cranks*, the other day.) I'm sorry things have been so hard for you lately, and I'd love to start a fan club.

That's all.

Subject: He's not hector mckerrow
Sender: bratbutt – 4.00 p.m. March 7

He's not Hector McKerrow! *I'm* Hector McKerrow! And if you wanna meet me, all you hot girlies, then check out my home page at www.lickspittle.com.uk/bollan.

Subject: Mercy you're a very nice girl
Sender: keyop.1 – 9.11 p.m. March 7

Mercy, you're a very nice girl. Please do *not* log on to bratbutt's home page, because he is not Hector McKerrow. I know *exactly* who he is, owing to the fact that Unus happens to be his service provider. I know his name, address, Mastercard number, and – more importantly – his age. I also know that he's a filthy-minded load of bollocks.

Yes, I am Neville Pratt. I don't want you thinking that

I'm Hector McKerrow. I'm also not a super-nerd, Britt – I'm a businessman. A *legitimate* businessman. So even if I could hack into the records of your Department of Social Security (which I can't), I wouldn't.

Please, will you girls be very, very careful? And will those people who've been e-mailing me about their computer problems kindly desist? Because I've no intention of replying.

Subject: Hey bratbutt – butt out
Sender: dunkndive – 7.30 p.m. March 7

Hey, bratbutt – BUTT OUT! You are one SICK ASSHOLE, man, I just looked at your website; you are a CREEP, boy. Pervorama.

Neville, can you access the Mastercard numbers of EVERYONE on the Net, or just Unus customers? (No wonder you're a millionaire!) Hey, if you can do a check on the whole Net, why not look for Hector McKerrow? Or Hector Johnson? You never know, he might be a user croozer.

God, I'm bored.

Subject: If you're looking for cards
Sender: supersupply – 9.02 a.m. March 8

If you're looking for cards, posters, photos, books or souvenirs featuring the greats of classic American TV and cinema, look no further. Write to Moviemania, 2/175 West 23rd Street, New York, NY. Or e-mail us on screenstuff@apex.mail.com.

Subject: I do not steal
Sender: keyop.1 – 1.00 p.m. March 8

I do *not* steal from my customers, Duncan! If you weren't so thick I'd employ my considerable resources to track you down and sue your pants off.

Subject: Just checking in
Sender: zinglebrit – 12.31 p.m. March 8

Just checking in, guys! Mercy, I think a fan club would be great – if I can be president. Slam, people like bratbutt aren't worth talking to. Neville, I'm like, wow. So cute, and such a *gentleman*. I saw your pic in *Web Guide*. Not exactly Hugh Grant, but almost. (If only you had the hair!) We own a Merc that's exactly, but *exactly*, like yours – same model, same color, same everything.

I was talking to a friend of my father's, last night – an old, old lawyer – and he said that he was on NBC's payroll when Hector punched out a camera technician who was hassling Hector's girlfriend, Rhonda. (He couldn't remember Rhonda's second name.) The whole thing was settled out of court, hush-hush, because NBC didn't want any negative publicity. This guy didn't seem to think much of Hector. 'Antisocial' was what he called him. With 'violent tendencies'.

I almost gave him a piece of my mind!

Subject: Mr mckerrow if you really are
Sender: mercynova – 4.42 p.m. March 8

Mr McKerrow, if you really are out there, and you happen to read this, I'm very sorry that it's gone so far. I just wanted to tell you how much I admire you, and ask if I could have an autograph. But don't worry – I won't try to contact you any more.

Subject: For those who are interested
Sender: quarxor – 9.13 p.m. March 8

For those who are interested, I followed Stephanie home from work today. She catches a bus. So now I know where she lives, and it's an apartment building, but I don't have time to stake the place out. Nor do I have the funds to bribe one of her neighbours. I dunno – I guess I was expecting to see Hector McKerrow kissing her on the doorstep, or something. I didn't realize what a tough job it would be, until I actually got there.

I spoke to her on the intercom, and asked for Hector, but she said I had the wrong address. I didn't even have the balls to come straight out and say something like: 'Have you ever been to the offices of Piggot, Crane and Warning?' But I did press some of the other buttons, and when I asked for Hector, no one said 'He lives in number twelve.' One woman told me that Stephanie lives alone, and that the guy who visits her (the guy who left that steamy message on her answering machine?) isn't anywhere near fifty – more like thirty/thirty-five – so that can't be Hector. *Or* Jerry.

If Stephanie does deliver Hector's cash, she must meet him somewhere to collect it. Or maybe she just gets it in the mail. Either way, it's a dead end for me. Isn't there some loser out there, like Duncan, who doesn't have anything better to do than stake out the lawyers' offices for the next two weeks, and see if Stephanie makes the drop?

No points for this. It's not getting us anywhere.

Subject: Up your ass mitman
Sender: dunkndive – 10.27 p.m. March 8

Up your ass, M.I.T.man. You're the loser. Whyn't you check out her trash? Too chicken, that's why. Too scared to get your dainty little Ivy League fingers dirty.

You think you're smart. You're not so smart. You should call up the lawyers. Tell 'em about Stephanie. Ask 'em if their receptionist remembers any skinny blonde who maybe comes in each month – maybe leaves an envelope?

Ah, you ain't got the guts. So maybe I'LL do it instead. Move OVER.

Subject: Perry hentze told me
Sender: swishy – 8.59 a.m. March 9

Perry Hentze told me what Britt told him – about this website? It's absolutely *outrageous*. I *love* it. And I see what you mean about Hector. I won't be missing another episode of *The Family Way*!

The reason I interrupted is because I once heard a story

91

about Hector from a very, very good friend of mine. A make-up artist. He told me that Hector once punched a hole in a mirror, and sliced up his hand. My friend was *terrified*. He'd been talking about plastic surgery, is all, and Hector (who was in the chair, having his lipstick applied) suddenly *exploded*! Well, I know my friend can be a little talkative, sometimes, but it's like a nervous tic – if there's a silence, he has to fill it. I guess I'm the same. And that's no reason to lose your temper!

Hector had to have stitches, and my friend practically had a heart attack. But Hector sent him a lovely book afterwards, on Cary Grant. (My friend adores Cary Grant.) Inside, Hector had written: 'Very sorry. I was in a bad mood. Hector'.

If you ask me, Hector was feeling a bit *sensitive* about his age. I think he was about forty, then, and that's when you start worrying about the old eyebags. Thinking about the nips and tucks.

It's certainly becoming an important issue for *me*!

Subject: Those goddam lawyers froze me out
Sender: dunkndive – 12.45 p.m. March 9

Those goddam lawyers froze me out, when I called 'em. Assholes. Probably cos I don't TALK right. Not an IVY LEAGUER. Pricks.

Hey Britt, whatsa matter with you? Neville's got a face like roadkill. Like a squashed skunk. Hugh Grant, my ass!

Sometimes I feel like punching mirrors myself.

Subject: Patty pryor just left
Sender: mousehound – 6.39 p.m. March 9

Patty Pryor just left. She knows a guy who knows a guy who owns Moviemania. He told her about this website.

She doesn't mind so much, but she said that if anyone tries to poke around *her* trash, she'll prosecute all of us.

She said that she told her lawyers about this website. She also asked them about Stephanie, but they said that the sealed envelope of cash from Hector arrives inside another envelope. It isn't dropped at the office. It's mailed, locally. In Boston. The handwriting on that envelope isn't the same as the writing on the one inside.

Patty said she doesn't like the idea that Hector's disappeared. She said that the lawyers had never told her about his old account being closed until I told her about their letter to Mercy. She said that she was afraid of Hector, because he'd always had a vicious streak.

She didn't say any of this to me. She was talking to my mom. But I heard them from my room, because the walls in our apartment are really thin.

My mom told me that I should stop using this website. So I guess I'll have to.

So long.

Subject: Are you guys aware
Sender: quarxor – 8.24 p.m. March 9

Are you guys aware that *TVNet* has voted this message board Site of the Week? Just thought you'd like to know.

Subject: Hector mckerrow
Sender: hadespy – 11.00 p.m. March 9

Hector McKerrow is dead. Let him rest in peace.

Progressing...

Subject: You won't believe this
Sender: mercynova – 5.45 p.m. March 10

You won't believe this, Adamina – I missed the end of last night's episode! My tape ran out! And it was such a good episode, too, because it was all about the measles. Dixie caught the measles, but only on one arm. You see, most of her bits had already been exposed to the measles, except her right arm, which became covered in spots. She felt just fine, except for the spots. But unfortunately she'd been invited to a beach party with the Jock Squad and some of her friends, so she begged Dr Devlin to find her a new arm. How could she wear a bikini when one arm was covered in spots? Of course, Dr Devlin said no. He said that she could wear long sleeves, and Dixie was devastated. Long sleeves at a beach party?

Meanwhile, Troy had caught the measles from Dixie. And when an alien catches the measles, you don't want to be around. First, his legs began to swell up, because he was sliding down to the bottom of his boy suit. Then, when he took off the suit, he turned bright red (instead of bright green), and his temperature soared. The whole house became hot, so hot that Zac and Dixie and Dr Devlin had to get out. Only Sylvia and the dog could stand the heat – Sylvia because she was a robot, and the dog because it was a very strange dog that never moved for *anything*. It just sat in front of the TV, and had to be force-fed.

Zac drove away on his bike, of course, but poor Dixie had to mope around the yard. She'd tried slathering make-up on her arm, but that hadn't worked. She'd thought of putting her arm in a cast, but didn't want to be wearing a cast for the rest of the summer vacation. So when Sandra looked over the fence, and asked her why she wasn't coming to the party, she told Sandra that she'd been grounded.

As for Dr Devlin, he was lost without his basement lab. He wandered around the neighbourhood, growling at people, until at last he decided to help out Floyd Johnson, who was glumly watering his wife's flowerbeds. Together they tinkered away, using some of Floyd's scientific equipment, until they fixed it so that the Johnsons' hose was able to water their flowers all by itself. Naturally, there were a few glitches in the design. When a pair of fire trucks screeched to a halt outside the Devlins' house, Floyd and Dr Devlin went to see what was going on, leaving the hose to attack Shirley Johnson. She was wearing a floral-print dress, you see, and the hose drenched her. (Ha ha.)

But what was going on at the Devlin's house? Well, Troy had begun to release clouds of noxious gas and steam, which were so thick that Sandra's mother, Mavis Peabody, had called the fire department. There was a lot of confusion (during which the dog remained sitting in front of the TV, tripping people up) but Sylvia managed to hide Troy from the firefighters by telling them that some chemicals in Dr Devlin's lab had exploded. Then, as the fire chief was talking sternly to Dr Devlin about dangerous chemicals and safety certificates and stuff, Troy began to float out of his bedroom window. He had turned into several big, luminous bubbles, the size of balloons. (As a matter of fact, I'm pretty sure they *were* balloons – because, as you know, the special effects in this show are pretty lame.) Some of the bubbles went one way, and some of them went another way. Sylvia chased the first bunch in her car, while Dixie followed the second on her bike, until she happened to run into Zac. They ended up at the lake, where Dixie's friends were having their 'beach party'.

And I don't know what happened next!

I don't believe that Hector's dead. I think it's another hoax. Hadespy, you ought to be ashamed of yourself.

Subject: Relax mercy
Sender: zinglebrit – 6.49 p.m. March 10

Relax, Mercy, I caught the whole episode. It was a bit over-the-top. At the beach, all of Troy's bubbles headed straight for Chet's battery-operated transistor radio, and sucked it dry of energy. They kinda *burst* when they did it, and became a big puddle of slime, which the kids thought was some sort of giant jellyfish. But Zac scraped it up, while Dixie, who was at the beach even though she'd said she was grounded, had to tell everyone about the 'poison ivy rash' on her arm. But everyone (especially Sandra) was so sweet about it that she realized it didn't matter after all. So she stayed.

The rest of Troy fastened on to a flashlight that Sylvia cleverly used to lure him down to earth. So he was taken back home, and put in the refrigerator, and pretty soon his temperature was normal again. That night the whole family sat down to dinner as if nothing had happened, until their motionless dog suddenly went mad, rushing around barking its head off, and disappeared out the front door.

Some dumb joke was made about it having the measles, and everybody laughed, just like in *Star Trek*. Not one of the better episodes, I've gotta say.

You know, I'm probably being stupid, but what if Hector *is* dead? What if somebody killed him? And what if whoever killed him doesn't want anyone to know about it (obviously), so he's paying the alimony to make it look like Hector's still alive? I mean, it would explain why no one can *find* Hector, wouldn't it.

Just a thought.

Subject: Maybe you're right
Sender: dunkndive – 10.59 p.m. March 10

Maybe you're right, zingle. Hell, what if it was a CIA hit? Hector bought stuff from Russia. His friend, Jerry, was supposed to have an 'activist background regarding government corruption'. What if it's all a cover-up?

WATCH YOUR BACKS, GUYS!

Mousehound, go tell your mom to piss in a sink. I mean it. We need you.

Subject: Britt you are one
Sender: vivala – 8.44 p.m. March 10

Britt, you are one sexy lady. I like Californian blondes. And I like a girl who can't run away when I chase her. *Woo-hoo!* Baby!

Sender: Invaders like you
Sender: keyop.1 – 12.31 p.m. March 11

Invaders like you, vivala, are the scum of the earth. You are *obscene*. Measures can be taken to block your entry, and they will be, if you soil this message board again.

Duncan, you're being ridiculous. A CIA hit, indeed. Why not go the whole hog? Why not alien abduction?

I can't tell you for a fact that hadespy is a fake. But it's interesting to note that he (or she) logged on at exactly the same time as our allegedly Spanish friend, Señor Croozer.

Mercy, now that this site has been widely publicized in *TVNet*, it's going to become the stamping ground of a great many drones, idiots and perverts. I really believe that you ought to close it down.

Subject: I guess you're right
Sender: mercynova – 4.28 p.m. March 11

I guess you're right, Neville. I guess I should close down. But not before I speak to Adamina. Adamina, I need your e-mail address, so I can keep telling you about *The Family Way*. Where are you? You haven't said anything for ages. For a week, in fact – I just checked. Are you on vacation, or something?

Subject: I work for
Sender: cinemex – 6.34 p.m. March 11

I work for New York's Museum of Television and Radio, and while it's gratifying to see so much interest displayed in a TV series deserving of far more attention, being, as it is, of unique and seminal importance, this persecution of an actor whose fragility has been amply demonstrated strikes me as *abominable*.

Hector McKerrow possessed a delicate talent largely derived from, and founded upon, his almost morbid sensitivity. Like Montgomery Clift, he depleted himself, physically and emotionally, with every performance; exposure of the sort required by the camera left him spiritually flayed.

I only met him once, many years ago, and was impressed by his all too evident struggle towards the light, which was carven upon his features. He was *immensely* delicate.

If you people have any respect for him as a man, as an artist, and as a person already tormented by the dark currents of mental illness, then *leave him alone*.

Subject: Jesus where are my
Sender: quarxor – 8.55 p.m. March 11

Jesus, where are my lecture notes? Hey, cinemex, why don't you quickly encapsulate the historiography of film noir, while you're at it?

Mercy, don't close this site. Don't you know you're a star? You were mentioned, *by name* in *TVNet*, as the creator of this 'amazingly addictive' site. How do you think you'll feel if you shut down, and someone else finds Hector McKerrow on another message board? Publicity isn't always a bad thing. Sure, you get a few psychos – but a lot more people are looking out for Hector McKerrow, now. He might be spotted any minute.

If his alimony's being mailed in Boston, then he's either living here, or sending it to someone (Stephanie?) who mails it for him.

Subject: Cinemex you don't know
Sender: Ierger – 6.30 p.m. March 11

Cinemex, you don't know what you're talking about. This guy – Hector McKerrow – has punched a mirror, assaulted a camera technician, thrown his girlfriend against a wall, and played ball with a plate of guacamole. And you're calling him 'delicate'?

If you ask me, he's a thug. I wouldn't be surprised if he *was* in some kind of a racket. In fact, I wouldn't be surprised if he'd killed somebody. *That* would be a good reason to keep a low profile.

Subject: OK i got a few things
Sender: dunkndive – 9.31 a.m. March 12

OK, I got a few things to say. First off, Neville, you're a piece of shit, but I'm with you all the way on vivala, that MUTHA! HEY! SCUMBAG! You think we dunno what you are, wormdick? You're a skinny little bug-eyed salami-slapper, and the only date you'll ever have is a dried one! You leave Britt alone, you asshole!

Second, if someone's killed Hector then Jerry Modder knows about it. He's got to.

The last thing is, what's everybody doin? Come on, Boston! Come on, Hollywood! We've stalled, here! Hasn't someone found another lead?

Subject: I've got another lead
Sender: sussy – 3.45 p.m. March 12

I've got another lead. I live in Sussex, New Brunswick, and this is the town where Hector McKerrow was born. I even know his mom – she lives near here. Every Christmas, he sends her a card. She doesn't know about this message board, unless she reads *TVNet*. I read it myself, which is why I logged on. Maybe I'll go tell her about it, though I don't know her so well.

Hector isn't dead. She would have heard, if he was. He calls her sometimes, but he never visits. My own mom used to teach Hector at school. Then he went off to Hollywood when he was sixteen, and only came back a couple of times.

His sister lives in Maine, somewhere. Her name's Iris.

Subject: So hector's canadian
Sender: mercynova – 4.41 p.m. March 12

So Hector's Canadian! And he's from the Maritimes, too! Oh my, this is so great. I can't wait to tell my sister. I wonder if Dad knows anyone from Sussex? The people at the base come from all over, and Dad's met most of them.

Adamina, where *are* you? I can't do anything until you talk to me!

Subject: Hey sussy do us all a favor
Sender: quarxor – 6.01 p.m. March 12

Hey sussy, do us all a favor, would you? Go talk to Hector's mom. Tell her what's going on. Ask her where the hell he is. And if she tells you, you'll win a clock radio.

Subject: Slam you are so sweet
Sender: zinglebrit – 5.17 p.m. March 12

Slam, you are so sweet. I'm like, totally touched. And Neville, too – thanks for looking out for me guys, but I'm OK. Really. If you're going to worry, worry about Adamina. I know it sounds stupid, but where do you think she is? I mean, when did she ever miss a chance to insult someone like vivala?

Gosh, I feel like a vacuum-head. Because guess what? I knew all along that Hector was Canadian! It says so on that CV his agent sent me. I just forgot. What a total, total wiener.

Sorry, guys.

Subject: Somebody should go beat the crap
Sender: hulk – 11.24 p.m. March 12

Somebody should go beat the crap outa that Stephanie bitch. Get her to tell the truth. I'd do it myself, if Boston didn't make me hurl.

Subject: Gee that's a real constructive
Sender: quarxor – 12.58 a.m. March 13

Gee, that's a real constructive suggestion. Piss off, ya big green goober.

Subject: Hello again everybody
Sender: mousehound – 10.27 a.m. March 13

Hello again, everybody. I guess I shouldn't be doing this. Mom will kill me if she finds out. But I wanted to tell you something.

Way back, I sent an e-mail to that magazine, *Enigma*, which is mentioned on Maynard Boyer's website. I asked the editor if he knew anything about Hector McKerrow, or the Free Thought Forum. Yesterday I got an e-mail back. The editor, whose name is Terry, told me that he'd received some correspondence from a Hector McKerrow about three or four years ago. He'd filed it away in what he called his 'wavie' file. (I don't know what he meant by that.) But he downloaded the letter, and sent it to me, and it's *exactly the same* as the letter posted by Egon Kucyk on his website. What's more, at the bottom of Hector's e-mail, there's a PO box number listed as his return address. He says that box numbers are more secure than the Net.

It's the same box number as Egon Kucyk's.

If you ask me, Hector McKerrow and Egon Kucyk are probably the same person.

Subject: Oh my god aaron
Sender: zinglebrit – 2.55 p.m. March 13

Oh my God, Aaron, do you think so? Oh, my God, that is so *totally cool*. Who's going to write the letter to that address? Do you want to, Aaron, or should we let Mercy? But if Hector replies, then you'll get the radio, guy. God, you're so smart.

It's like a *race* between you and sussy. I can't wait to see who wins! (But I hope you do, mouse.)

Subject: Gee i don't know
Sender: mercynova – 7.10 p.m. March 13

Gee, I don't know. I don't think I want to write to that post-office box. It's all a bit – I don't know – kind of creepy. Can't someone else do it?

Nobody out there's heard from Adamina, have they? I mean, on e-mail or something like that? You haven't, have you, Neville?

Subject: I'm sorry to say that
Sender: keyop.1 – 11.15 p.m. March 13

I'm sorry to say that I haven't heard from Adamina, Mercy. But I'm sure she's all right. Maybe she's got a lot of homework. And if she *is* sick – well, it probably isn't serious.

Has it occurred to you that all those very expensive calls she made to America might have resulted in disciplinary action? Like no phone calls, for instance? And no modem, either?

Adamina, if there is something wrong, you've got my e-mail address. (And no crank e-mails, please, because I have ways of sussing you out.) Aaron, well done. I don't approve, but I have to say that you're *remarkable*.

Subject: Come on sussy
Sender: lerger – 9.13 a.m. March 14

Come on, sussy, get moving. Where are you, at church? I found that PO box number on the Net, and I'm writing to it myself. Anybody object?

Subject: Yes I do object
Sender: zinglebrit – 12.18 p.m. March 14

Yes I do object! Who the hell are *you*, anyway? *I'll* write the letter, if Mercy doesn't want to. Adamina, if you've got a problem with that, you'd better say something. But even if you did write, it would take, like, *weeks* to get here, right? I mean, from Australia? So it's better if I volunteer – since Neville disapproves and Aaron's mom would probably freak out.

Slam, we haven't heard from you, lately. What's going on?

Subject: My money's on sussy
Sender: sleepr – 4.11 p.m. March 14

My money's on sussy. And the suspense is *killing* me.

Subject: I visited with mrs mckerrow
Sender: sussy – 7.30 p.m. March 14

I visited with Mrs McKerrow, today. Told her what was happening, but I don't think she took it all in. She's pretty old, you know. Needs looking after, I reckon.

When I asked her where her son was, she said she didn't know. Said he wouldn't tell her – just 'moves around a lot'. Doesn't call on his sister. I didn't push her, because she got upset. Made me feel bad, if you want to know.

Hector sure was a good-looking guy. Pictures of him all over the place. Magazine pictures, mostly. There was an old one of him with Jack Lemmon.

Sorry I can't help you guys. Looks like Hector's keeping a pretty low profile.

Subject: People if his mom doesn't know
Sender: quarxor – 9.30 p.m. March 14

People, if his mom doesn't know where he is, then something's wrong. This guy is on the run. I mean, gimme a break, you know? He sends her a Christmas card but she doesn't know where he is? Only someone on the lam would act like that.

Sussy, did it occur to you to ask his mom about

postmarks? Did that even cross your mind? I sure hope so.

If Hector McKerrow is using an Albany post-office box, like Aaron said, then how could he be living in Boston? He must be mailing his stuff to Stephanie.

Anyway, I'm gonna write him. I've served my time on this message board, I don't care what anybody says.

May the best user win.

Subject: Hi everybody
Sender: s.o.inoz – 5.36 p.m. March 15

Hi, everybody. Sorry about the prolonged silence. I guess the best explanation would be that I got a bit shat off with life in general and . . . sort of . . . I dunno, took time out. Lay in bed. Went for walks. Wagged school. You know. Bit of a bummer, but this message board keeps me sane, and there's light at the end of the tunnel. They're talking about sending me to a shrink, and that would be good, because I want to be a shrink when I 'grow up'. What a great job! Sitting around all day on a big, comfy chair, listening to people's juicy little secrets.

Anyway, I won't bore you with the details of my tedious life. I just wanted to share something with you, because I think it's pretty important. The thing is, I haven't been wasting my time, this last week or so – I've been ploughing through all the stuff that Aaron's been ploughing through (Aaron, please don't disappear), and some extra stuff that he might not have bothered with. *Very* tenuous links. A few lucky shots. And what I've worked out is this.

Hector McKerrow is a 'wavie'.

What, you may ask, is a wavie? Well, apparently every

senator and congressional representative in the US has a 'wavie' file. Wavies are people who say that they're victims of 'clandestine bombardment with non-ionizing radiation' (accord to some UFO expert called Martin Cannon). They reckon that they're harassed by computer-generated music, noises and voices delivered into their minds via microwaves from a satellite, and that this harassment – and surveillance – is carried out by various corrupt corporations and government departments. There's one guy, I checked out his website, and he says that an advanced computer is reading his thoughts, and transmitting them to the media, so that some of the TV announcers say what he's thinking *right after he's thought it*. Also, his house gets buzzed by helicopters. Also, ambulance sirens wail when he goes to the toilet. Stuff like that.

Loony, or what?

These people are paranoid. I mean *paranoid*. They think the whole world is out to get them: police, media, politicians, businessmen, everyone. They think that every move they make, and every word they utter, and every thought they think, is being monitored. So what would *you* do, in the circumstances? You'd try to get away, right?

Hector tried to get away. He tried to get away in Tasmania – but it didn't work. My guess is that he was still hearing voices (or whatever) in Strahan. You can run but you can't hide, you know? Not when you're suffering from a severe case of schizophrenia.

Anyway, he disappeared. He changed his name, he dropped out of sight, and he bought one of those spark plug things. Those 'Novoton Biocorrectors'. Why? Because Novoton Biocorrectors are 'a high technology defence against harmful electromagnetic radiation'. My bet is that he hasn't had any problems since he bought one of those things, because if he had, he wouldn't be putting so much effort into disappearing. Why bother, if he knew that his movements were being plotted from outer space?

This is what I think, and I bet it's the truth. My friends, I'm afraid that Hector McKerrow is off his noodle. I hate to say it – I *really* hate to say it – but he's a nutter. So is Jerry Modder, probably. God, it's so depressing.

Anyway, this means that we're harassing someone who's mentally ill. Like cinemex said, it's not on. Neville was right. It isn't fair. We should stop *now*.

Thanks for worrying about me, Mercy, but I'm OK. Really.

Subject: I'm so sorry that things have been tough
Sender: mercynova – 4.59 p.m. March 15

I'm so sorry that things have been tough, Adamina. I wish I could help. But you didn't give me your e-mail – I can't close this message board unless you give me your e-mail. Or don't you want to hear about *The Family Way* any more?

I guess you must be right about Hector being a 'wavie'. It sounds awful. I wish I'd never started this stupid site.

Subject: Adamina please don't post
Sender: keyop.1 – 9.04 p.m. March 15

Adamina, please don't post your e-mail. You know what Britt's had to put up with, lately – and you should see what's been popping up on *my* mail since I posted my address. If Adamina sends her address to me, then I can send it on to you, Mercy, and it won't become public property.

I've said it before and I'll say it again: *please* will you girls be careful? You'd be just as safe hitchhiking as you would broadcasting your e-mail address all over the World Wide Web. You've no idea how manipulative people can be.

On the subject of Hector McKerrow, I believe that Adamina is bang-on. (You're a clever girl, Adamina.) As a consequence, it should be stated that anyone who wishes to pursue the poor man henceforth, whether on this site or any other, is a blood-sucking, bollocks-for-brains *ghoul*.

Subject: Go piss in a bag
Sender: dunkndive – 11.00 p.m. March 15

Go piss in a bag, Neville! And don't you DARE close this board, Mercy, you dumb Canuck! What does Adamina know? Nuthin! She's got no proof, for Chrissake! OK, so Hector might be a wavie – but he might be a terrorist, too! Can't you see that? If you close this site, I swear, I'll open another one in five minutes flat! Because you know what? I reckon old Hector's *lurkin*. I reckon he's logged on. I reckon he's got his ear to the gear, because I'm in Albany, right now (came down yesterday), and I've staked out that PO box from *5.00 a.m.* and no one's gone *near* it! No one! It's like he *knows* we know. You know?

Listen, Hector. There's one way to stop all this, and it's up to you. Make contact. That's all you gotta do. Just make contact. Tell us what your problem is. You can't be traced on the Net. There's no need to be scared.

Hell, if I were you, I'd be goddam *flattered*.

Subject: Mercy i know how you feel
Sender: zinglebrit – 12.34 p.m. March 16

Mercy, I know how you feel – if it's true about Hector, it's way depressing – but for once I think Slam is right. What if this 'wavie' business is just a front? And if it isn't, then what if we can help poor Hector? And – oh, I dunno, it just wouldn't feel right, closing the board now. It just wouldn't.

Don't you think we should at least *vote* on it?

Subject: Hear hear
Sender: quarxor – 3.17 p.m. March 16

Hear, hear. Let's vote on it. I vote we leave the site open – at least until we work out the point scores so far. *Someone's* gotta win that clock radio.

Subject: You people are ignorant fools
Sender: moniter – 5.35 p.m. March 16

You people are ignorant fools. You know nothing of the powers that control our world today. You know nothing of the suffering inflicted on innocent people by institutions that defend their corrupt and covert practises with secret inhuman technologies, effectively rendering their victims powerless beneath the label 'loony' or 'extremist'. What do you know of the Bio-pacer III, which can produce a number of mind-altering frequencies without being attached to the subject – or subjects? What do you know of the Alpha-stim, TENS, the Synschro-energizer, Tranquilite, etc?

In 1984, a neo-Nazi group that called itself The Order offered $100,000 to a pair of government scientists in exchange for information about the clandestine research they were engaged in. What was this research concerned with? Only a plan to project chemical imbalances and render targeted individuals docile via particular frequencies of electronic waves!

As long ago as the 1930s, F. Cazzamilli was researching the effects of electromagnetic waves on the human nervous system. (He found that one frequency caused a ringing in the ears of his subjects, who also wanted to bite the scientists involved.) Other experiments have shown that people can hear and understand spoken words delivered through a pulsed-microwave analogue of the speaker's sound vibrations. And these are only the experiments we know about! For years, the Soviets bombarded our Moscow embassy with microwaves. Who knows what the US government is doing to its own citizens today?

The wavies know. They have experienced it. Yet their complaints are dismissed as the 'ravings' and 'hallucinations' of 'madmen'. Although they are harassed and persecuted, few will try to help. And those who do are persecuted in turn.

You people should familiarize yourselves with the true dimensions of this problem. You should open your eyes to what's going on around you, and stop condemning the victims of harassment as 'loonies'.

One day, when the privacy of your own head is invaded, you'll know just how powerful the forces are that have ranged themselves against freedom and individualism.

Subject: Hector
Sender: mercynova – 6.45 p.m. March 16

Hector? Is that you?

Neville hasn't heard from you, Adamina, so I guess I'll post the next episode. It was a weird one. Zac was in trouble because he'd fixed his motorbike to make a noise like a police siren when he drove it, forcing everyone to get out of his way. Naturally, the police had something to say about that. So Dr Devlin ripped the gadget out of Zac's bike, and Zac got mad, and drove off in a huff. Then he ran into a bunch of bikers, and made friends because they admired all the custom-built stuff on his machine.

Meanwhile, Troy was also in trouble because Dr Devlin had found all his test tubes and things in a heap on the floor. Troy said he didn't do it, but no one believed him. They locked him in his room, but he took off his boy suit and got out, slurping through a crack in the windowsill. Dixie discovered that he was gone when she came to bawl him out for putting all her make-up on the dog. Oh – this time the dog was perfectly behaved. Or so it seemed.

Troy was blamed for doing other things, too, like turning up the oven so high that Sylvia's cookies were burned (she had to feed them to the dog), and for drawing whiskers on Zac's pin-up of Marilyn Monroe. But they couldn't say 'good riddance to bad rubbish', because Troy was at large without his camouflage suit. So Dr Devlin went looking for Troy in his car, and Dixie went looking on her bike, and Sylvia went looking around the neighbourhood. She talked to Sonny, but Sonny hadn't seen Troy. And Dixie talked to Zac, who was with some of his biker buddies, but Zac hadn't seen Troy either – and refused to help look for him.

Then Sonny went to his favorite hideout, and found Troy there. When he called the Devlins' house, however, he was told (by a gruff voice) that Troy wasn't wanted any more. Since Troy said that he didn't want to go back either, there was nothing much that Sonny could do.

Finally, all the rest of the Devlins (except Zac) returned to their house. They were trying to make the dog sniff one of Troy's sweaters, and track him down, when Sonny looked over the fence and asked them what they were doing. He was amazed to find out that they were still looking for Troy. 'But I called the house, and someone told me that you didn't want Troy any more,' he said. Then Sylvia said, 'Who told you that? There was no one here, this morning.' Then Dixie said, 'Except the dog,' And they all looked at the dog.

At that moment, Zac came limping back home. His bike had been taken by drunken bikers. Needless to say, the Devlins weren't going to put up with *that*. So they got hold of Troy, and piled into the car, and went and slugged it out with the bikers, who just weren't a match for an angry robot, a glowing green monster from outer space, and the fact that Zac could order his bike around by remote control. It wasn't much of a fight, really.

As for the dog, they got rid of it when they realized that it had been sabotaging their happy home, smashing test tubes and answering telephones and stuff. Like I said, it was a weird episode.

Do you think – I mean, that message last night – do you think it could have been Hector?

Subject: It could have been anyone
Sender: quarxor – 6.18 p.m. March 17

It could have been anyone. Anyone with only half a brain,
I mean. Obviously there's a whole buncha mad wavies out
there.

Sussy, you haven't answered my question about the
postmark. Slam, has it occurred to you that people don't
necessarily collect their mail every day? Like, what if he
does it once a week? What if he does it at midnight? A
crazy like Hector probably only goes when it's dark.

Hey – maybe he's a vampire.

Subject: I vote we keep this board open
Sender: lerger – 10.30 p.m. March 17

I vote we keep this board open. That's two for, and two
against. Who else is gonna vote? Britt? Slam?

Subject: Do you people have no compassion
Sender: keyop.1 – 9.02 a.m. March 18

Do you people have no *compassion*? No *sense*? Hector
McKerrow would be quite justified in taking legal action
against you – have you thought of that?

Adamina, my dear, you must have misspelled your
e-mail address. Mercy can't get through on the one you
gave me.

Subject: I heard you the first time
Sender: sussy – 1.10 p.m. March 18

I heard you the first time, quarxor. Sure, I asked about the postmark on Mrs McKerrow's Christmas card. She said it came from Boston, Massachusetts. So maybe Stephanie is mailing Hector's Christmas cards, too.

I don't wanna butt in, or nothing, but it would be pretty hard to sue anyone on this site. Even if you could find out everybody's name, how could you prove that it was really them logging on? It's like with the voting. That's a dumb idea. I could sit here and log on as half a dozen people, with six different votes, and who would know it?

There's just one more thing I wanna say. If anyone starts bugging Mrs McKerrow, I'll come and knock their eyes out.

Subject: Like i said
Sender: dunkndive – 5.30 p.m. March 18

Like I said – Hector's tuned into this site. Codename: moniter. Mercy was right. I KNOW that message was you, my man. That's why I'm back in Syracuse, cos you're too smart to collect your mail while I'M around. You're way too smart for that. In fact, you're way too smart to be a headcase at all.

Hey, I know this wavie stuff is horseshit. Like Britt said, it's a front. No one's gonna bug you if they think you're screwy, because, like who'd be such an asshole, right?

Wrong. I vote we keep this board OPEN – until someone

tracks you down. Whatever you've done, you're gonna pay for it in the end, man.

Listen – I dunno about the resta you guys, but I had to give this portal crew my e-mail address when I registered to log on. Isn't there some way we can get *moniter's* e-mail off their database? C'mon, Neville, you must be buddy-buddy with these E-write people. Can't you do it?

Subject: For your information
Sender: Keyop.1 – 10.00 p.m. March 18

For your information, sussy, it's easy enough to sue a server. I know. It almost happened to my company, once – because one of my clients wasn't behaving himself. I was asked to stop servicing that particular client, and I wasn't about to argue. However unlikely the risk of legal action might be in the slippery world of the Internet, most companies would rather avoid the possibility altogether.

If Hector chooses to lodge an official complaint, I doubt that Mercy's server will be any more courageous that Unus was.

Slam, even if I could get moniter's e-mail adress from E-write (which is doubtful, frankly), there is no guarantee whatsoever that the e-mail address given by moniter – if, indeed, he gave one – was genuine. There's really no way of screening these things. And if moniter *is* Hector, why on earth would he reveal his e-mail address?

Subject: For those wishing to
Server: cinemex – 8.11 p.m. March 18

For those wishing to pay homage to Hector McKerrow without persecuting him, I have instituted my own 'Classic TV' website at http://www.fabnet.program/.com. It covers certain unique series such as *The Family Way*, *Operation Petticoat*, *The Odd Couple*, *Ozzie and Harriet*, *The Many Loves of Dobie Gillis* and *Beauty and the Beast*. I have collected a gallery of photo stills and some interesting texts, including TV schedule listings, promotional material and interviews. There is also a letterbox, for those who wish to comment. (Constructive comments *only* please; certain people of a vindictive and thoughtless character are *not* welcome.)

Subject: Reading through this message board
Sender: slurpee – 5.45 p.m. March 19

Reading through this message board, I see that the pommy bloke has managed to cosy up to all the teenage girls who log on. He's even got hold of their private e-mail addresses, I notice. Like 'em young, do you, mate?

Subject: I'm a reporter
Sender: hots – 8.59 a.m. March 19

I'm a reporter working on *Hots* magazine, which is aimed at the youth market. We have a 'Latest' section which looks at current trends, popular clubs, new fashions, rising stars, hot websites, etc. I want to ask Mercy Whetton a couple of questions about this message board – unless she intends to close it down before our May issue hits the street. If not, could she please tell me:

1) What other actors/musicians/TV shows does she like?
2) Has she set up, or participated in, any other Internet message boards or websites?
3) How many hours a day does she spend on her computer?
4) Can she download a photograph of herself?
5) What impact does she think computers have had on teenagers in North America?

If you could post answers to these before Monday, Mercy, I'd appreciate it. We've got a deadline.

Subject: Oh wow
Sender: zinglebrit – 12.33 p.m. March 19

Oh wow! Mercy! You really *are* famous! God, I've *seen* that magazine! One of my friends actually *subscribes* to it!

Hey, you can't close the board now. And miss out on all this media coverage? What if *I'm* mentioned? Please, please don't pull the plug – not yet. I'll give you my original *Ten Commandments* movie poster, if you don't.

By the way, in case *Hots* is interested, I'm sixteen, I spend about four hours a day on my computer, and I think that computers have had, like a *huge* impact on teenagers in North America. You wouldn't believe how many chat rooms I'm involved in. For someone like me, who can't get out much, it's just the best thing. You make all kinds of friends. And I know a lot of kids who'd rather log on to a website than go to a party. I even know some kids who have Internet parties! They all sit around with their computers and have a great time!

Also, there are so many boys who are addicted, and I mean *addicted*, to computer games. It's, like, worse than drugs.

Anyway, that's my opinion. For what it's worth!

Subject: To the reporter
Sender: mercynova – 4.44 p.m. March 19

To the reporter from *Hots*: I can't download a photo. I don't have the right gadget. But Dad says that if you post your real name, he'll buy a copy of *Hots*, and send my picture to the address in the magazine. That way, we'll know if you're really a reporter, he says.

I guess I'm not like a lot of other kids, because I'm not into Leonardo di Caprio or *NSYNC or stuff like that. I like Gene Wilder in *Willy Wonka and the Chocolate Factory*, and I like Anthony Perkins (who was in *Psycho*), and I like the Rankin Family, and Elvis Presley, and *Green Acres* (I love Eva Gabor). Oh, and I like *The Simpsons*, and Sean Connery. And the guy who plays Sherlock Holmes in an English TV series, but I can't remember his name.

I don't spend too long on the computer, because it's Dad's computer – and my sister uses it, too. So I'm not like Britt. I'm not involved in many chat rooms. All I do is, I like to check out *The Simpsons* sites. And this site too, of course. Mostly this site. It's the first one I ever set up.

Britt is probably right. Computers probably have had a big impact on the kids in North America. Most of my friends have them, and use them to write up their home-work and stuff. They're great for that. And for playing games in the winter, when there's nothing on TV.

I've decided I won't close this site. Not yet. Not if you want to do a story about it. But I don't want anyone chasing Hector McKerrow any more. I just want to talk about the shows he's been in, and what a good actor he was. If he *is* logging on, like Slam says, then I want him to feel good about how many people love his work.

Maybe then he won't try to sue me or stuff like that. He won't, will he? I'm a fan, is all. But if he does complain to this server, I'll close the site.

Subject: I'm going to respond
Sender: keyop.1 – 9.48 p.m. March 19

I'm going to respond very, very quietly and calmly to slurpee and his insinuations (although they deserve to be ignored) because, thanks to the intrusive nature of this website, everyone now knows who I am. I don't want any rumours flying about which might damage my reputation. Also, I don't want any of my younger Internet friends to be alarmed.

Mercy and Adamina will both, I believe, testify to the fact that I have not made use of their e-mail addresses. I have sent some material to Mercy through the post, at her own request, and did not enclose so much as a business card. It appears that I am the only responsible adult who logs on to this message board, and therefore feel the need to urge caution on those young girls who have *no idea* of the repercussions of careless Internet usage.

127

Girls, I'm a father. I have one son and one daughter, and though I don't get to see them very often (they live with their mother, as you will know if you've read that wretched *Web Guide*), I do as much as I can to ensure that they're safe and happy. You'll find that, once you're parents, all children will become objects of concern to you.

Speaking of which: Adamina, I got that e-mail address, and have passed it on to Mercy. As I said, I won't be using it myself. Your parents probably wouldn't like it if I did.

Subject: Gimme a break
Sender: dunkndive – 7.50 p.m. March 19

Gimme a BREAK. Maybe out in fantasy land every kid's got a computer, and, like, half a million goddam *Carmageddons* and shit, but here in Syracuse, where I live, there are PLENTY of kids whose dads can't even bankroll a microwave, let alone a computer. Hell, most of the Gameboys they use are stolen. The heapa junk *I've* got somebody threw out. And a guy I know fixed it for a coupla bucks. (That's his story, anyway.)

I gotta hand it to you, Mercy – you got some guts. *Willy Wonka and the Chocolate Factory*? If the kids at your school find out, you'll be hunkered down in closets till you leave junior high.

128

Subject: Neville i know
Sender: s.o.inoz – 2.02 p.m. March 20

Neville, I know you're not a sleazebag. Some people have dirty minds. And I would have e-mailed you to tell you not to worry, if I could have been bothered scrolling through this message board again to find your address.

As I've mentioned, my dad hardly ever sees me (like you hardly ever see your daughter), and I know for a fact that he's not out chasing underage bimbos, either on the Internet or anywhere else. How do I know this? Because he's made of iron ore and basalt. All he cares about is his next shareholders' meeting.

Mercy, your morals are crumbling in the face of worldly temptation. I'd send you an e-mail to this effect, only I'm not really penpal material. I can hardly dredge up any interest in my own life, let alone anybody else's. Try mailing Britt or something, if you want to chat. Neville's probably got her address. (Just kidding, Nezza!)

Oh – and Neville? You could download pornographic *death threats* on to my e-mail, and no one around here would give a flying fart.

Subject: Is the poll
Sender: swishy – 10.57 a.m. March 20

Is the poll still in progress? Because if it is, then I want to vote that you all leave Hector alone – for your own sakes. I told you what he did to my friend's mirror. It's pretty obvious that he *shouldn't be crossed*.

129

Subject: If you're interested
Sender: epi – 2.12 p.m. March 20

If you're interested in tracking down Hector McKerrow, I can help, for a fee. I'm an information broker, and I make a living on the Internet. If Hector McKerrow is an American resident, and has ever registered to vote, I can dig up his address and date of birth. With these two pieces of data (which are a matter of public record) I can provide court records, medical records, credit history, annual income, phone numbers, whatever. You name it. It's all available through the Net, and it wouldn't take more than half an hour for each item.

Without his *current* address – which is obviously what you're looking for – I'd have to work backwards a little, and it would cost more. But I'll find him for $50.

Anyone wanting to discuss this with me should e-mail me on epi/dowser@apex.mail.com for payment details, etc.

Subject: I would urge you all
Sender: keyop.1 – 7.28 p.m. March 20

I would urge you all *not* to contact that broker. These people are often very dubious types. I know – I've had dealings with one or two.

Adamina, I'm so very sorry. I won't e-mail you (on principle), and it wouldn't be appropriate to discuss the matter here, but isn't there someone you can talk to? My dear, you clearly have so much to offer, but you're terribly unhappy. I wish there was something I could do to help.

Subject: Come on guys
Sender: quarxor – 11.11 p.m. March 20

Come on, guys! Can't someone spare $50? *I* can't – I can't even afford decent razor blades – but I know Neville could. Neville, man, loosen up! You've obviously shelled out a bit of cash on some previous occasion, or you wouldn't have had 'dealings with' brokers before. What were you doing, trying to track down your ex-wife? Is that why you don't see your kids much? Because she's lying low? What did you do, beat her around the head with a keyboard?

Adamina, you sound like you could use a few drugs. Prozac, for instance. Or a line of cocaine.

Subject: What is this
Sender: s.o.inoz – 3.50 p.m. March 21

What is this? Suddenly everyone's worried about my mood. Neville, I'm not unhappy – I'm a realist. Quarxor, I should have known that you were a dealer. It wouldn't surprise me if you were hunting down Hector yourself, because he owes you money. Wouldn't that be an interesting twist?

'Information broker'. That's an impressive-sounding euphemism for a sleazy job. Personally, I never buy *anything* over the Net – not even information. It gets so people know too much about you.

Subject: That's a stupid thing
Sender: mercynova – 10.43 a.m. March 21

That's a stupid thing to say, quarxor! You shouldn't be talking about taking drugs! Do *you* take drugs? If so, you're *really stupid*. Adamina, don't pay any attention. Drugs don't solve *anything*.

Subject: Once again i'm obliged
Sender: keyop.1 – 2.55 p.m. March 21

Once again, I'm obliged to correct certain *misapprehensions*. I have never employed an electronic private investigator for *any* purpose – *certainly* not to locate any of my family, with whom I am on perfectly cordial terms. As Adamina quite correctly pointed out, personal information can be collected over the Internet, and information about purchasing habits is particularly valuable to information brokers, as well as to the companies that buy from them – companies that, generally speaking, want to direct their marketing at specific targets. My own company has been approached by information brokers on several occasions, looking for data about some of my clients whose Internet habits have been carefully monitored.

Quarxor, I'd take offence if it wasn't perfectly obvious that you were drunk – or stoned – when you wrote your last message.

Mercy, my dear, you're quite right. Drugs don't solve anything.

Subject: You know on reflection
Sender: quarxor – 4.00 p.m. March 21

You know, on reflection, I don't think this board is really my scene. The Bible-belters seem to be taking over.

'Drugs don't solve anything.' Jeest! Try telling that to a diabetic.

Subject: Attention
Sender: lerger – 2.30 p.m. March 21

Attention! I'd be ready and willing to chip in a few bucks towards that fifty. Anyone else wanna cough up? Come on, guys, five dollars each. It's not much to ask.

Subject: Speak for yourself
Sender: dunkndive – 8.09 p.m. March 21

Speak for yourself, lerger. Five bucks might not mean much to you, but it's a HELLUVA lot to some people. When I was in Albany, I paid this old bum $5 so he'd sleep all night in front of Egon/Hector's post-office box, and he did it. No problem.

You're crazy if you send off five bucks to some faceless private dick's bank account. How do you know he's gonna deliver?

133

Neville, you're totally going to *freak*, I know (and Slam is, too!), but I couldn't resist it. I contacted that broker. It's a she, not a he. And I gave her my credit card number. And now she says it's a 'bigger job than she thought', because Hector's been changing his name so much, and she wants another $50! She's good, though. She got his records from that psychiatric hospital he was in, and then she used them to access his medical insurance payment records, and from those she found out his bank account details (when he was living with Perry Hentze) and his credit history, and then she was *really* clever, because she found out that he'd been using the name 'Johnson'. Without me telling her! And when she put Hector Johnson together with an Albany address that was listed after the LA one, in his insurance records, she got a new credit history. Hector Johnson had a credit card, see: he bought his Novoton Biocorrector with it (well, done, Aaron!), and was a bit slow with the repayments. It hasn't been used since, though: she said he must be dealing in cash, now. She said he's a tough one. She said that Hector Johnson has really worked at covering his tracks – not like Hector McKerrow. She said that he must have faked up some kind of ID, with maybe a fake social security number. Then I mentioned Egon Kucyk, and she said she'd look into it.

According to her, everything she does is legal, and Dad says so too. He says that all the big companies use people's medical and credit records for lots of different stuff. (I'm starting to think that Hector isn't quite so paranoid after all!) Anyhow, I'm sitting here waiting for the next instalment, kind of wondering if I'm doing the right thing, but it can't be legal, can it? I mean, Hector using fake ID?

Slam, why did you pay someone five dollars to sit in front of Egon Kucyk's PO box?

Subject: So you've got your own credit card
Sender: s.o.inoz – 12.48 p.m. March 22

So you've got your own credit card, have you, Britt? Figures. And it looks like you're going to *buy* your way to the finish line. But I guess I can't very well be jealous, can I? Of a handicapped person, I mean.

If I were Slam, I would have picked the shaggiest, smelliest tramp available to sleep in front of Hector's post-box. That way I would have scared Hector off from collecting his mail in the middle of the night.

Not a bad idea, Slam. Not bad at all. You've got a brain, if you'd use it constructively. But no – you have to spend your waking hours making life even more miserable for a guy who must be *considerably* more depressed than I am, poor bastard.

By the way, I've had a perv at *Hots* online (you can't get the printed mag, here), and I think it's the biggest load of rancid tripe I've ever had the misfortune to lay eyes on. In case anyone's interested.

PS Britt, of course you didn't have to tell your information broker about the name Johnson. She only had to read this message board, you dork.

Subject: Thanks for your comments
Sender: hots – 9.34 a.m. March 22

Thanks for your comments, s.o.inoz. I'll be sure and convey them to my editor.

Mercy, my name is Peta Purchese. Thanks for taking the time to answer my questions; I'll look out for your photo. Please remember to include a return address with it, if you want it back.

Subject: Christ but adamina
Sender: heptroll – 9.00 a.m. March 22

Christ, but Adamina is a sour bitch. What's her *problem*, for God's sake?

Subject: People like you
Sender: quarxor – 12.15 p.m. March 22

People like you, I should think. *Heptroll*? Jesus!

Subject: Please britt please
Sender: mercynova – 4.11 p.m. March 22

Please, Britt, *please* don't take this any further, I'm begging you. It makes me feel so bad. Please. Don't you care about Hector at *all*? I thought you liked him. Think how skinny and sad he always was. Honest, I can't stand it. I really can't. Please, can't you leave him be? Why are you doing this?

Subject: Ok i'm out of it
Sender: dunkndive – 7.09 p.m. March 22

OK, I'm OUT of it! OUT! *OUT*! Shat on! Picked up! Are you happy? 'Get your ass out of here,' they said, 'or we'll take you down to the station!' LOITERING, the pricks, and I was doing sweet FA! Yeah, that's right, in ALBANY. I've been in Albany all along, stakin out that goddam pissed-on chewed-up ASSHOLE POST OFFICE. I woulda had him, I know it, he thought I was back in Syracuse and now I AM back in Syracuse, because of those stinkin lousy bastard cops, they NEVER LEAVE ME ALONE!

This system sucks. THIS SYSTEM SUCKS! I've had it. I HAVE HAD IT! You can all go to hell – the cops especially!

Subject: Take it easy
Sender: s.o.inoz – 12.01 p.m. March 23

Take it easy, Slam. It was a good idea, but it was a long shot. You don't know if Hector's really monitoring this board. And you don't know if he's still using that post-office box.

I know it's tough, getting hassled all the time (do you dress like a junkie, or something?) but just remember: there are no police on the Net. So relax.

Subject: I'm logging on
Sender: mousehound – 3.50 p.m. March 23

I'm logging on with my mom's permission. Patty Pryor
didn't get her alimony this month. She wants to know if
it's because of you guys?

She's pretty mad about it. She says if the money doesn't
show by the end of the month, she'll start legal proceedings
against just about everybody.

I guess this could mean that Hector's been lurking, huh?
Maybe he's scared of paying, in case someone traces him.
Maybe he's scared that someone's staking out Stephanie's
house, or the lawyers' office.

If he is tuned in now, like Slam says, then my advice is:
pay over that money, Hector! Fast!

Subject: Oh no
Sender: mercynova – 4.49 p.m. March 23

Oh no! This is bad! Britt, did you get my message? Have
you stopped that broker? Will everyone please stop? Listen
– if anyone out there is spying on Stephanie, or the
lawyers' place, or the PO box, then *stop right now*.

Subject: Hah
Sender: dunkndive – 7.15 p.m. March 23

Hah! What did I tell you? Of COURSE Hector is logged
on! HEY! HEY, HECTOR! I knew it all along, man! Why
don't you come out and say a few words?

I think I find Hector McKerrow for you – no charge.

I watch *The Family Way* a couple times (I'm a shift worker, see) and I like it. Well, one day I visit my uncle, he got rooming house here in Johnstown (NY), and I see this guy, a roomer, calls himself Egon, older guy with gray hair, but I keep thinking 'He look familiar, to me.' So I say to him 'I know you?', and he say 'No'. Then, next morning – foop! Gone. Without paying board. My uncle is very angry, that happen three days ago, meanwhile I'm thinking, thinking, I watch *The Family Way* and – there! Egon! At least, maybe it's Egon. I tell my son, then, and he say to me 'Dad, everyone looking for him!' He tell me about this crazy website, show me, and we see the name, Egon Kucyk.

Pretty good, uh? Also, I got his car for you. White Mercury Lynx, maybe '81, '82, first three letters of license plate, RVS.

Do I get radio, now?

Subject: Hold on a minute
Sender: quarxor – 10.45 a.m. March 24

Hold on a minute. OK, so we know where Hector was three days ago, but we don't know where he is *now*, do we?

I thought the clock radio was for an address where we could reach him. We can't reach him in Johnstown any more.

Subject: Exciting huh
Sender: zinglebrit – 5.12 p.m. March 24

Exciting, huh? Wow!

I got an e-mail from 'my broker' last night (I've just been checking) and she says that Egon Kucyk was born in 1946, died in 1954. She says that dead people's birth certificates are often used to get fake ID. (I wonder what name Hector's car is registered under?) She says she can't find anything else about Egon Kucyk yet – but I guess we know that someone *calling* himself Egon has been in Johnstown, recently. Why Johnstown, I wonder? Sounds like Hector's on the run.

Mercy, I promise I'll fire that broker. If Hector's stopped paying alimony, then we should all just let him be. (Believe me, we *don't* want to get mixed up with *lawyers*.) By the way, where are you? Did you miss last night's episode of *The Family Way*? Or did you e-mail your update straight to Adamina?

I'm about to watch it myself, so if you missed it, I can easily tell you what happened.

Subject: This is sgt ralph harrelson
Sender: police – 9.38 p.m. March 24

This is Sgt Ralph Harrelson, from Greenwood RCMP, Nova Scotia. Would anyone out there having any knowledge about the current whereabouts of Hector McKerrow please telephone me on 0011-1-902-812-6800. Mr McKerrow is wanted in connection with an assault last night in this area.

We're interested in talking to 'fannick' regarding Egon Kucyk and Egon Kucyk's car. Also to 'sussy', urgently.

Subject: God help us
Sender: s.o.inoz – 4.00 p.m. March 25

God help us, what's happened? Mercy? Are you there? Will somebody please tell me what's going on? What does RCMP stand for? Is it an army thing? Nobody's answering when I dial that number – but then it must be about one o'clock in the morning, over in Greenwood. Would there be something in the local paper? What *is* the local paper, around there? Would it be online? I can't even get CNN!

Oh, *shit* this!

Subject: All right now everybody
Sender: keyop.1 – 12.15 p.m. March 25

All right now, everybody keep calm. I'll see what I can find out on the Net. I just rang Harrelson's number, and it turns out that he's a policeman (RCMP stands for Royal Canadian Mounted Police) but I was asked to leave a message, so maybe he'll call me back.

Subject: I haven't seen anything
Sender: zinglebrit – 8.05 a.m. March 25

I haven't seen *anything* on CNN, I watched it for over an hour last night, and there was nothing on the NBC news either, but then I guess we don't get much about Canada here. Will someone from Canada *please* tell us what's going on? I'm about to call Harrelson right now!

Subject: Sounds like you guys didn't hear
Sender: sussy – 12.55 p.m. March 25

Sounds like you guys didn't hear what happened. Well, that's no surprise. I didn't work it out for myself, when I saw the ATV news last night, because they didn't mention anyone's name. But I just called up the RCMP, like they asked me to, and that hold-up in Greenwood, night before last? That was Mercy Whetton's family. They say Hector McKerrow did it. Threatened 'em all with a gun, tied 'em up in the basement, and made off with a whole bunch of stuff from their house. Crazy, eh? Poor kid. And poor Mrs McKerrow.

I guess the Mounties will be heading her way soon.

Subject: For god's sake sussy
Sender: s.o.inoz – 7.30 a.m. March 26

For God's sake, sussy, what *happened*? Who got assaulted?
Was it Mercy? What did the police need to know? Have
they got him yet? What on earth did he *want*?

Jesus, I feel like I'm stuck down the bottom of a *well*,
here!

Subject: Adamina there's nothing you can do
Sender: keyop.1 – 10.00 p.m. March 25

Adamina, there's nothing you can do, so you might as well
calm down. Mercy's not hurt. Her father was struck on the
head, but the wound wasn't serious. Just a cut. When
Sergeant Harrelson returned my call, he told me that
Hector McKerrow arrived at the Whettons' house on
Tuesday night, at about eight thirty. Hector was there for
five or six hours, mostly talking to Mercy's father and
searching the house. He drove off in the Whettons' car,
taking their computer, some books, and various disks and
files with him. The car was found abandoned not far
away, but it was empty. Hector must have parked his own
car some distance from the house.

The family weren't discovered in their basement until
about ten or eleven o'clock on Wednesday morning.
Physically, they were all right. Apparently Hector had
gagged them, but had given them all a dose of nasal
decongestant, so they wouldn't suffocate. According to the
police, he must have brought the nasal spray with him.
And the tape he used to tie them up.

They haven't found him yet. There's a fellow I work with who comes from Nova Scotia, and he says that, by ten or eleven o'clock, Hector could have been out of the country. He says that two or three hours away from Greenwood there's a place called Yarmouth, where you can catch a ferry to Portland, Maine.

The police weren't very forthcoming. They seemed a bit suspicious of me, and you can't blame them. I'm sure they're suspicious of anyone associated with this message board, which is to blame for *everything* that's happened. They wouldn't tell me what Hector wanted. They wouldn't promise to pass on my good wishes and sympathy.

I'd like to e-mail Mercy, but it's probably not a good idea. Adamina, I'm sure that you could do it without causing offence. Perhaps I'll just send a card. Poor little girl. How terrible. How absolutely awful.

This is what comes of *tormenting a sick man*!

Subject: Mom says i shouldn't
Sender: mousehound – 7.20 p.m. March 25

Mom says I shouldn't log on, but I just watched the news, and Mercy's name was on it. They had footage of her house, but not of her. Only the back of her father. I guess she doesn't want to talk to anybody.

If you do check out this board, Mercy, I'm really sorry about what happened. My brother's nanny got held up in a convenience store once, and she was so upset that she was off work for nearly two weeks.

Subject: Just a message of sympathy
Sender: imput – 7.40 p.m. March 25

Just a message of sympathy to the poor little girl who was
on TV. Guns are a terrible curse.

Subject: Goddam
Sender: dunkndive – 9.04 p.m. March 25

Goddam. This is heavy, huh? Are you OK, Mercy?
GodDAM, what did I tell you? Hector's *bad*, man! I bet
that gun's not even registered! Why do you think he did it?
Do you think he wanted the computer so Mercy couldn't
log on any more, or some dumb idea like that? Maybe he
wanted her to shut down this board – except, in that case,
why didn't he just make her do it? The board's still here. I
don't get it, do you?

I understand if you don't wanna talk about it yet,
Mercy, but if you told us what happened, then maybe we
could help. I mean, I bet we know more about Hector
McKerrow than the cops do.

Hey, he's not gonna be able to hide out for long. Now
he's all OVER the news, man, he's everywhere! TV STAR
HOLDS FAMILY AT GUNPOINT! If that guy, that
fannick – if *he* recognized Hector from *The Family Way*,
then everyone else will too. I mean, I saw the clips and
pictures they showed on TV. He's a good-lookin guy. And
his eyes – you couldn't mistake his eyes. And his voice.

The cops should stake out Jerry Modder's place. And
Stephanie's. I'm gonna call and tell 'em.

God, Slam, you are such a total *dipstick*! Like Mercy would really want to talk to *you*. Like she'd want to have anything to *do* with this message board!

Adamina, they still haven't found Hector. Like Slam said, it's all over the news now – I guess it wasn't really news until someone realized that an American actor was involved (except that he's not American). Has the story reached Australia yet? I guarantee they'll move *The Family Way* to a 7.30 p.m. timeslot. And I guess they'll do a piece on *E!* or *Hard Copy*, or something. And I feel *so bad*, because it's all my fault! I mean, I bet if I hadn't hired that broker, none of this would have happened!

Have the police contacted that broker yet? I bet she can help them.

I can't believe what I've been missing! This is a *great* board. Hey, this *is* the website they were talking about, right? On the news? It's gotta be.

Cool!

Dear Mercy,

I am very sorry for what I did. I just read your journal – your little story – because when I found it, hidden behind your wardrobe, I thought that it might contain evidence. I was in a hurry, you see, and I saw a locked box, and naturally I assumed that it might be of relevance to me. To my problem. So I took it.

I've just spent the last two days searching through your father's files and correspondence. It's taken me a long time, because I'm not very proficient on computers. I didn't find what I was looking for. And then, when I read your little story, it became clear to me, somehow – I don't know why. Suddenly I realized that you were telling the truth, you and your father. Suddenly I realized that he *hadn't* been using your name on this message board, in an attempt to flush me out of hiding, because this journal is really yours. I can see that. And I'm so very sorry, so very, very sorry.

It's not your father who's directly to blame for what's happened, nor his superiors, not even the Canadian army. I would never have found any proof of persecution in your father's files, because there was no proof to find. Instead – and I should have realized it – the culprits are those executives who chose to broadcast *The Family Way* again. Influenced by the forces arrayed against me, they clearly hoped to manipulate people like you, Mercy – innocent children – to find me for them. What other explanation would there be for disinterring that old and foolish series? I should have known. I should have understood, the moment I saw your family getting into your car, on Tuesday morning. I hadn't really believed that you existed, until then. I had thought that you were an invention of the conspirators who are seeking me out. And I might have turned away, and gone to find my true tormentors, if I hadn't seen your father's uniform. It was the uniform that misled me. I have a great distrust of uniforms. Naturally, I assumed that you were lying because your father had told you to.

Mercy, I would never have hurt you, or your family. Not seriously, I mean. Forgive me for striking your father. I'm afraid that I'm a little – I can lose my temper – I get angry so fast, and it's wrong. It's bad. And I thought he was lying, you see, because he wouldn't admit to what he actually didn't do. When I – that is, when things are over, I'll tell you where to collect your computer and your journal.

I signed the last page for you, though perhaps you won't want my autograph now. In fact you probably won't want the journal any more, because it's so full of me. All those pictures – I can't believe you found them. Some of them so old. It's terrible to think that I've destroyed this lovely fantasy. (I was in love with Rita Hayworth, when I was a boy.) But at least I received your letters, Mercy. At least I read all the wonderful letters you wrote me in your journal. I know that you wanted to send me a letter, because I've been keeping an eye on this message board. I was the one who told you that I was dead. That I was in Spain. If only you'd all believed me, this would never have happened! If only you'd left my friends alone!

Mercy, I hope you read this. I hope you receive my apology. I'm so ashamed, because what I did to you, and to your father, and to your mother, and to your sister, is the worse thing I've ever done. And you tried to tell me, when I was in your house, but I wouldn't listen. I wouldn't believe you.

Well, you won't see me again. Things seem to be drawing to a close. But before I sign off, just a word of advice. It wasn't hard for me to find you, when I reached Greenwood. All I had to do was look in the local directory. Neville is right – you should be careful when you use the Internet. Very careful.

And so should everyone else.

Subject: Hey
Sender: wzzzzz – 11.14 p.m. March 25

Hey! Freak me out! It's the *man*! Hey, love your stuff, guy!

Subject: Hector if you're reading this
Sender: s.o.inoz – 7.05 p.m. March 26

Hector, if you're reading this, *please* don't do anything stupid! I mean, you're going to give yourself up, aren't you? I'm sure the police will take into account the fact that you're – well, that you've been in a psychiatric institution. That you're *emotionally fragile*, I mean. That you're under a great deal of stress.

I can't believe this is happening. And I was just about to hand in my Media Studies assignment! I can't use *The Family Way* now. It would be so *crass*.

Subject: Far out
Sender: dunkndive – 8.30 a.m. March 26

Far out, uh? Listen, there must be some way to trace that
message. (Is it really Hector's, Mercy? You'd know. I
mean, about the journal and all.) Can't the cops trace it
somehow? Them and this network? Neville, get off your
ass, man! You MUST be able to help!

I told those Canucks about Jerry Modder, and they
wanted his ADDRESS, Britt, for your information! So
maybe I'm not such a dipstick after all.

Stay tuned, cos I'll have CNN on all day. Maybe they'll
give us some updates.

Subject: I told you
Sender: cinemex – 9.11 a.m. March 26

I told you! I told you what would happen! On your heads
be it! You're *obscene*! You've driven this man over the
edge!

Subject: I'm looking for comments
Sender: LouiseHayter – 10.02 a.m. March 26

I'm looking for comments to feature in a story I'm doing
on Hector McKerrow, which has been commissioned by
People Weekly magazine. Will Britt, Aaron, Neville,
Duncan, Adamina and 'quarxor' please call me on 212-63-
4574. Mercy, I'd especially like to talk to you, though I
understand that you're not doing interviews, right now. If

you want, we can talk over the Net. Right here, maybe. Or my e-mail is LouiseH@haytercom.com.

Subject: I called the cops
Sender: quarxor – 10.20 a.m. March 26

I called the cops with Stephanie's address. Maybe *they* can get something out of her.

You know, I bet Mercy could make big bucks selling this to *Hard Copy*. In fact, nobody should say a word to the media without negotiating a price first.

I know I'm going to, when I call that reporter from *People Weekly*.

Subject: Quarxor you are disgusting
Sender: keyop.1 – 4.25 p.m. March 26

Quarxor, you are disgusting. Adamina, have you managed to contact Mercy? Hector, if you're reading this, please ask yourself: for what reason have TV stations been re-running episodes of *The Addams Family*, *Star Trek*, and *My Three Sons* for the last ten years? It wasn't to uncover the whereabouts of John Astin or Leonard Nimoy. Please understand that you're overreacting. You need help. And the longer you elude the authorities, the less help you're going to receive when they track you down.

Subject: Can't you see what's happening
Sender: moniter – 12.40 p.m. March 26

Can't you see what's happening? You're playing into their hands, all of you! Hector isn't overreacting, he's trying to expose the *truth*! And you won't listen! No one will listen! Proof is what's needed – proof that even the sceptics can't deny. Otherwise, thousands of innocent people will continue to suffer.

You don't know what it's like – the mental torment. Have you no compassion? If Hector surrenders himself, they'll know where he is for years and years to come. How can he escape them in custody? He can't. His protection will be removed, his sleep will be invaded, his thoughts will be monitored – unless the people of the United States demand an investigation into how supposedly dormant facilities are being accessed to destroy the lives of people like Hector.

Please contact the White House and voice your concerns. Only with your support can the victims of microwave harassment at last receive the kind of attention and sympathy that they deserve. Technology is killing us.

Subject: Has anyone else been tuned into
Sender: dunkndive – 2.00 p.m. March 26

Has anyone else been tuned into CNN? If you haven't, I just saw Jerry Modder! No shit! They musta tracked him down from THIS BOARD, man, thanks to ME, and staked out Champs. When he showed up at the store he really let 'em have it, boy, that guy's got MOUTH.

Sounded like a crazy man. Told 'em they were media whores, in the pay of NASA and the US defense force and I don't know whatall (I mean, some headcase)! And there was this guy on the show, this shrink or professor or some shit, and he was talkin about 'wavies' and it was just like Adamina said. Woof! Did we ever open a can of worms!

Subject: I just heard a rumor
Sender: zinglebrit – 12.01 p.m. March 26

I just heard a rumor from one of my friends (whose dad's a producer) that Jerry Springer's looking to do a show on 'wavies', which is *so* tacky, I mean *please*. Can you imagine? '*My brain is a radio receiver, and the State Department's doing the programming*.' Springer must be running around like a headless chicken, looking for paranoid schizophrenics.

You know, has it occurred to anyone that for Hector, who after all was in show business, it mightn't be too hard to track *me* down? The blonde paraplegic daughter of a lawyer who works for Universal Pictures? Hollywood's a pretty small town, you know. I mean, supposing Hector thinks it's *my* fault, now? Because I hired that broker?

I'm going to talk to Dad about calling in some security. Did you hear that, Hector? Just in case you've got any weird ideas. Our house is like Fort Knox anyway. You'd never get past the camera on the front gate.

Subject: You assholes
Sender: lendo – 3.05 p.m. March 26

You assholes. You bunch of assholes. Look what you've done now.
   May you rot in hell.

Subject: What do you mean
Sender: s.o.inoz – 7.20 a.m. March 27

What do you mean, lendo? What *have* we done? Are you talking about poor Mercy, or has something else happened? There was nothing on the seven o'clock news, television *or* radio. Please will someone post an explanation?

Subject: May god have mercy
Sender: cinemex – 4.33 p.m. March 26

May God have mercy on his soul.

Subject: You people ought to be ashamed
Sender: triplay – 4.50 p.m. March 26

You people ought to be ashamed of yourselves.

Subject: Get real
Sender: quarxor – 5.20 p.m. March 26

Get real, will you? He was a *lunatic*, for Chrissake! We're not responsible if he wants to blow his head off!

Yes, that's right, Adamina, he's blown his head off. On camera, for all to see. He baled up some television executive called Phil Frugoni in an underground parking lot in New York, then shot himself through the skull when the cops arrived. It was all on one of those security cameras, and someone must have sounded the alarm.

The footage wasn't too good. I mean, black and white. Fuzzy. Couldn't hear the words, just the voices. Even so, we'll probably be seeing it about 3,000 times a day for the next week.

You know how the media loves an on-camera shooting.

Subject: Adamina
Sender: keyop.1 – 10.36 p.m. March 26

Adamina? Listen to me. You're obviously monitoring this board, and in case you don't read your e-mail, I want to give you the telephone number of a woman I know, a lovely woman. She's a counsellor and I've talked to her about you, so if you want to get anything off your chest, you can reverse the charges. She'll accept; I've arranged it with her. Or you can e-mail me your telephone number and she'll ring you, but perhaps you don't want to do something like that. Or perhaps you can talk to your mother. Or to one of your teachers.

Do you understand? I'm concerned about what's

happened, and how it might affect you. I don't know you at all, really – there's every chance that you're a middle-aged bank manager – but I think you are who you say you are, and I think that you might need some help. Because it's a terrible thing that's happened. A terrible, terrible thing. I feel so bad about it myself, and I'm sure that you must feel shocking.

Mercy, my dear, if you ever happen to read this, please don't be too upset, because you're not to blame. I know you're probably being well looked after, but anything I can do, anything at all, you know where to reach me. I'm so sorry. So very sorry. It shouldn't have turned out like this.

Subject: Hector mckerrow
Sender: moniter – 7.15 p.m. March 26

Hector McKerrow is a martyr. Hector McKerrow's death has brought to the world's attention the plight of those who seek Freedom of Thought. Certain covert departments and research institutions have his blood on their hands.

He will not have died in vain. Some day, everyone will know who really pulled that trigger.

Subject: Oh god
Sender: zinglebrit – 4.30 p.m. March 26

Oh God, he's dead! I don't believe it! Oh God, and he was so beautiful! This is just – this is so – do you think it's our fault? Do you think it's really our fault?

Oh God, I can't even watch. It's everywhere, over and over again. I didn't mean it. It was like a computer game, it didn't seem real. Poor Hector! I'm so sorry! There must something we can do. Isn't there something we can do? I'm just *sick*, I feel so awful!

Dad says that Phil Frugoni is a programming director with Nickelodeon, and that he and Hector were acquainted. So maybe Hector was asking Phil – at gunpoint – for proof that there was some sort of conspiracy. I mean, proof that it was the Defense Department's idea to run *The Family Way*, or whatever. And then, when the police came, Hector didn't want to be taken alive, poor thing. God, it's like a movie, I bet HBO makes a movie out of it, and we're all the bad guys. Unless they make it into a thriller, and pretend that there really *is* a conspiracy. Then we'd just be, like, pawns. Puppets. Only maybe one of us could find out what was really going on, and join forces with Hector? That way you could have someone young and spunky to co-star with the older actor.

God, look at this. I sound like such a jerk. Comes of living in LA, I guess. But it *is* a good idea, don't you think? And it would be a kind of monument to Hector.

There goes my mobile. It practically hasn't stopped, the last hour. Everyone's like, *hanging* off this message board. They think I'm so cool, because I was in at the beginning.

Bye.

Subject: Of course it's not our fault
Sender: lerger – 6.45 p.m. March 26

Of course it's not our fault that Hector blew his brains out. Like quarxor said, he was crazy. People like that are always trashing themselves.

Subject: I guess i was wrong
Sender: dunkndive – 8.20 p.m. March 26

I guess I was wrong.
   Shit.
   I dunno. Maybe I should just stick to computer games. Every time I try to make a difference, things always turn out worse. What a dumbass punk I am.
   Sorry, Hector. It wasn't personal.

Subject: Neville i can't find
Sender: s.o.inoz – 1.30 p.m. March 27

Neville, I can't find your e-mail address, this board is so big. Can you send me *your* phone number, please? Instead of your friend's?
   I think I'd prefer to talk to you, if that's all right.

Subject: I thought you all should know
Sender: mercynova – 8.00 a.m. March 27

I thought you all should know that a fax arrived at my father's office, today. It was from Hector. He must have got the number from Dad's computer files.

It gave me the address of the Fire Island summer house that he was hiding in, when he logged on last night. He said that our computer and stuff are all there, and he gave me the name of the man who owns the house, which is only used in the summer. One of Hector's friends, I guess. But he didn't know Hector was there, according to Hector. They hadn't spoken in a long time.

The reason I thought I should mention this is that Hector said something else – something you might want to know. He said: 'It's possible that one or two of your Internet friends may have been "planted" to keep the search going. But for the most part, I believe them to be innocent of any malicious motive. Like you, they are simply fans of mine. So I don't bear them any ill will.'

Maybe he thought this would make everyone feel better. It doesn't make *me* feel better. When you see stuff on TV, you don't realize . . . I mean, you don't understand what it's really like. Not really. Not until it happens to you.

I'm closing this message board, now.

It's the last time I'll ever be looking at one.

Subject: Yes it's the new
Sender: lerger – 7.45 p.m. March 28

Yes! It's the *new* Hector McKerrow message board! For all you people who still want to know what in hell's going on, I've started this board to keep you posted.

For example, you might want to know:

a) Exactly what Hector wanted from Phil Frugoni (yet to be revealed by the media – has anybody else heard anything?)

b) Exactly where was Hector's Fire Island hideout, and did he leave a suicide note there?

c) What's Mercy Whetton doing these days? Where is she now? What did Hector say to her, on Tuesday night? This I *really* want to find out.

Come on, guys! Let's have some feedback!

Subject: I wish i'd logged on
Sender: ozmate – 8.08 p.m. March 29

I wish I'd logged on sooner – I mean, before they closed down the last board. Because it turns out that s.o.inoz is the same Adamina who lives two houses away. I worked it out about a week ago, when it suddenly hit me: how many other Adaminas can there be in Sydney, who wear Doc Martens and have hairy armpits and whose parents are divorced?

And now I know for *sure*, after she went running down the street on Friday night, bawling her eyes out, and sort of collapsed outside our front gate. My dad went out to see what she was up to, and then he took her home, and her mother was there, and they had to call a doctor. She was a real mess. Upset, I s'pose – about Hector McKerrow. Anyway, she came around this morning with her mum, to apologize for freaking out on our doorstep, and to thank my dad for being so helpful, and I asked her straight out if she was s.o.inoz. She sort of glared at me (she's a really scary-looking girl, you know, really tough-looking, I reckon she's got tattoos) and she said 'What if I am?' And then her mother said that her (Adamina's) psychiatrist was handling things, it was all the fault of the Internet, and she was going to make sure that Adamina didn't use the Internet any more. Boy! Did that piss Adamina off! She turned around and she said to her mother, 'Try and stop me.' And her mother said, 'Addy, you shouldn't be communicating with those people. They're deficient personalities.' (Hi, all you deficient personalities, out there!) So Adamina said, 'Well, what do you think *you* are?' – was she ever mad! – and her mother said, 'Don't talk to me like that!', and next thing they were having this huge argument! Right in our lounge room!

Adamina kept saying that Neville wasn't a deficient personality, that he'd been great, better than her own dad had ever been, and if it hadn't been for Neville, she would have *really* flipped out. And her mum kept saying he was a stranger, they didn't know him, until finally Adamina said that she did know him, she'd spoken to him on the phone, even though he didn't want her to because her parents didn't approve, but she'd done it anyway because he was the only adult she knew who talked any sense. And she said that if her mother didn't let her phone him up and discuss what happened, she was going to take out all her savings and fly to England. So there.

Anyway, that was when the whole thing wound down, because Adamina's mum was too embarrassed to hang around any more. Pity. I would have liked to know what they decided to do. But it looks to me like Adamina's made a friend.

Which is good, when you think about it, because she never seemed to have any before.

Too much of a bitch, I guess.

Subject: Listen you assholes
Sender: dunkndive – 9.30 a.m. March 29

Listen, you assholes. You leave those girls alone, do you hear? LEAVE THOSE GIRLS ALONE. Do what you like with Hector, he's dead anyway, but Mercy and Adamina are OUT OF BOUNDS. You ain't gonna bother 'em, you ain't gonna talk about 'em, you're gonna LAY OFF. They're REAL PEOPLE, you dumb jerks, they're not blips on a computer screen, and they don't deserve what you wanna dish out.

Don't mess with their lives.

Hey Mercy, if you're tuning in – what kind of gun was Hector using on Tuesday night? I'd really, really like to know.

John Marsden
Letters from the Inside

Dear Tracey
I don't know why I'm answering your ad, to be honest. It's not
like I'm into pen pals, but it's a boring Sunday here, wet,
everybody's out, and I thought it'd be something different . . .

Dear Mandy
Thanks for writing. You write so well, much better than me. I
put the ad in for a joke, like a dare, and yours was the only
good answer . . .

Two girls begin a friendship – two strangers exchanging letters,
getting to know each other a little better every time they write.

Sometimes writing's easier than talking. Secrets and fears seem
safer on paper. And both girls have plenty of each – fears they
hardly dare to confront; secrets that could blow their lives apart.

John Marsden
Tomorrow When the War Began

Hell isn't only a place for the damned.
Sometimes it's a place where the saved take refuge.

Seven teenagers take a trip to Hell.
And seven return. To find Hell has come home.

It takes one week to escape from civilization and live rough in a
remote, unexplored valley. It takes one week for civilization to
be destroyed.

Now there is only one place to hide . . .

John Marsden
The Dead of the Night

*There was a crashing sound from the bushes. I spun round,
wondering if this was my death, the last movement I would
ever make, the last sight I would ever see . . .*

Their country has been invaded. Their homes have been
occupied by strangers. Their families are facing death at the
hands of a merciless enemy.

Only one group of teenagers – fugitives in a remote valley – will
never give in. Whatever it costs them.

The second book in an electrifying series about lives, changed
forever in a world at war.

Terence Blacker
Homebird

*Beneath the headline is a picture of a wild-eyed kid, a broken
bottle in his hand – crazy, violent, the stuff of parents'
nightmares.*

You guessed it. The Bottle Boy is me.

Nicky Morrison's parents have big plans for him. Wanting him
to be successful and conventional, they send him away to
boarding school. But a few weeks later, Nicky is on the run.

Trying to make sense of his world, he joins a group of squatters.
The freedom they offer seems just what he needs. But their
leader, Scag, has sinister plans for Nicky. Soon his life is slipping
dangerously out of control, and so is his chance of ever going
home again . . .

Peter Dickinson
Eva

Eva wakes . . .

She has been in a coma for eight months after a horrifying
accident. She hears her mother murmur, 'It's all right. You're
going to be all right.' But there's something terrible in the voice.

Eva has changed. From now on she must live a life that no one
has ever lived before. A life that will change the world.

Philip Pullman
The Broken Bridge

Ginny is sixteen, and life is great . . .

She's turning out to be a brilliant artist like her mother, who died when she was a baby. She loves her home by the sea. Best of all, Andy has come back for the summer, but Ginny's world is about to break apart.

Her father has kept a devastating secret from her all her life. Piece by piece, she discovers that everything he has told her about herself is a lie. So who is she? Ginny must return to the dark tragedies of the past to find out.

Jaclyn Moriarty
Feeling Sorry for Celia

ELIZABETH!!! LOOK AT THIS NOTE!!
OVER HERE!!! ON THE FRIDGE!!!!!

Hope you're feeling better. If you're dead, ring me. I'm at an emergency meeting of the poetry club.

I want to make you a special lemon soufflé. The recipe is in the bottom drawer – you're welcome to begin it anytime.

(And see if you can think of a slogan for raspberry-flavoured cat food)

Love – your thoughtful
and considerate
MUM

P.S. Have you heard anything from Celia yet?

A selected list of titles available from Macmillan Children's Books

The prices shown below are correct at the time of going to press. However, Macmillan Publishers reserve the right to show new retail prices on covers which may differ from those previously advertised.

John Marsden		
Letters from the Inside	0 330 39776 1	£4.99
Tomorrow When the War Began	0 330 33739 4	£4.99
The Dead of the Night	0 330 33740 8	£4.99
Terence Blacker		
Homebird	0 330 39798 2	£4.99
Peter Dickinson		
Eva	0 330 48384 6	£4.99
Philip Pullman		
The Broken Bridge	0 330 39797 4	£4.99
Jaclyn Moriarty		
Feeling Sorry For Celia	0 330 39725 7	£4.99

All Macmillan titles can be ordered at your local bookshop or are available by post from:

Book Service by Post
PO Box 29, Douglas, Isle of Man IM99 1BQ

Credit cards accepted. For details:
Telephone: 01624 675137
Fax: 01624 670923
E-mail: bookshop@enterprise.net

Free postage and packing in the UK.
Overseas customers: add £1 per book (paperback)
and £3 per book (hardback).